George Thomson and the Deadly Quest

K.G. Dolling

Applied M&B Publishing

A CIP catalogue record for this book is available from the British Library.

ISBN-13: 978-1-8382454-0-5

Published worldwide by Applied M&B Publishing, Burton on Trent.

kevin.dolling@btinternet.com

Cover design by It's Great To Be Rich, York.

Printed and bound in Great Britain by Inc Dot Design & Print, York.

Dedicated to Diane and Charlotte,
for always believing in me.

And to George my mentor.

CHAPTER 1

George and the Vanishing Ribbon

Have you ever felt like you don't quite belong?

It's hard to put a finger on how you're feeling.

Everything appears to be the same. Your nose is still in the middle of your face, you still have two ears, one on each side of your head. You should be where you are, everyone expects you to be there, you are not actually out of place. However, something just doesn't quite feel right.

You're wearing the right clothes for the occasion, you're neither late nor early, no one is taking any particular notice of you, but you still feel like you have a big neon sign on your head saying 'I don't belong here'.

So what do you do? Go and hide in the corner and hope the feeling will go away, or try to carry on regardless, hoping no one will notice and 'catch you out'?

Do you ever get these feelings?

George often gets these feelings. He can't explain why he gets them; he doesn't understand them, and let's face it, as a fourteen-year-old boy, how could he?

He doesn't have the worldly experience to fully understand his feelings and it's hard enough coping with the physical and emotional changes everyone goes through at that age without feeling like he is a stranger from a different world.

All George wanted was to be a normal boy. To grow

up with his mum and dad, and live a normal life with his friends and the rest of his family. Like any kid of his age, he longed for adventure – but the kind of adventure you can have in the garden and still be home for tea!

It was early June, and so far, the day had started like any other early summer's day. The sun was trying to break through the clouds, birds were chirruping and you could hear the sound of neighbours talking to each other as they climbed into their cars ready to set off to work.

Like so many other days, George had woken up to the sounds and the smells of his grandma making breakfast, the sound of the radio playing, the clink of the cups in their saucers, the clank of the spoon stirring in the sugar. Then, best of all was the smell of hot buttered toast drifting up the stairs.

Gran never had any trouble getting George out of bed, as he loved his food and was soon up and ready when the smell of the warm toast wafted into his bedroom.

Right, thought George. *I need to get down there before Granny gives my breakfast to the dog, but first she will make me sort out my bed and go and have a wash – so some quick thinking is required, George my boy.* With a quick pull on the duvet and a bash of his pillows his bed was made – well, it was as good as it was going to get when George was doing it.

Thank heaven Gran has changed from those old blankets and sheets, he thought. It had taken him most of the morning to make his bed when he first moved in with his grandmother. He had never heard of 'hospital corners' until he lived with his gran. *No wonder people struggle to get better in hospital*, he thought, *if they all have to make their beds with hospital corners every morning, I'm surprised some haven't starved to death while trying to make their bed with hospital corners!*

Chapter 1 – George and the Vanishing Ribbon

Although Gran looked after him very well, she did tend to be a little overprotective and she did insist he did his chores about the house. 'It will make a man of you,' she used to tell him when he complained about doing his chores.

The first chore of the day was making his bed, followed swiftly by a wash, teeth cleaned, hair combed and getting dressed, and all before he could get stuck into his breakfast!

Right, bathroom now, George said to himself. Racing into the bathroom, he grabbed his toothbrush in his left hand, quickly squeezed a small drop of toothpaste onto the brush and stuffed it in his mouth. Picking up his hairbrush, George frantically scrubbed his teeth with one hand while he pulled and tugged at his hair with the brush.

Throwing the hairbrush back into its box and putting the toothbrush back into its holder, he spat out the toothpaste into the sink and poured some cold water through his hands. With a flick of his hands he threw the water at his face, grabbed the towel and gave his face a hard scrub. 'Done!' he shouted. 'Now for breakfast.'

George made a dash for the bathroom door. In a skip he was at the top of the stairs and in just four bounds he had reached the bottom, almost falling flat on his face into the bargain.

'Mornin' Gran,' he said, as he burst through the kitchen door and slid straight between his chair and the kitchen table.

'Good morning, young man,' replied his grandmother. 'I trust you slept well? Are you ready for some tea and toast, better to eat up while it's still warm.'

'Am I ever!' said George, as he grabbed his tea mug in one hand and started layering slabs of butter onto his

7

toast with the other.

'What do you have planned for today?' asked Gran.

George thought quickly, his mind racing with ideas that Gran would consider 'worthwhile'. He knew if he hadn't got a full itinerary planned, his Gran would try to fill his day with chores, and no one likes doing chores when there are adventures to be had!

It was the weekend, mid-June. George had arranged to meet his best friend Charlie later that morning, so his 'getting out of chores' excuse was all primed and ready.

'Err, out with Charlie,' he exclaimed. 'Busy day! Lots to do, Gran. Definitely no time to do any chores, although you know I'd love to, but just far too busy. Sorry, Gran.'

He buried his head into his tea mug and hoped the matter was solved.

Gran gave him a knowing look. She knew he would prefer to be out playing, but George is a good boy and she knew he would help out if she really needed his help.

June was a significant month for George. He spent most of his time thinking of his parents Dominic and Lucy.

Last summer, he had been just a regular kid growing up with his mum and dad in their little village buried in the heart of rural England, nothing unusual in any way. Dad worked in a building society and mum ran a small internet business out of the spare bedroom, mainly to give her something to do, and it helped to bring in a little extra cash.

The cash came in handy to pay for holidays and the little extras like takeaway pizza once a week and ice cream or a cake in town when they went shopping on Saturday. His life, though not completely full of fun and adventure, was happy and full of love. However, as things drifted on week by week, George was totally unaware that his idyllic 'normal' life was about to change.

It all started on 18 June last year, when his life suddenly turned from humdrum but happy to a complete unthinkable nightmare. He had woken up exactly the same as he always did, to the sound of his Batman alarm clock. He could hear his mum downstairs preparing breakfast and his dad making singing noises in the shower. He slid out of bed and into his slippers, wiping sleep from his eyes. Standing up, he grabbed his dressing gown off the back of the chair and wandered downstairs. The usual pleasantries were exchanged before Dad appeared all clean and ready for work. Breakfast was eaten with the usual chatter:

'What are you doing at work today, dear?'

'Will you be late home?'

'Have you remembered your packed lunch, George?'

'Walk quickly to school and don't hang about.'

George left for school on foot. It was only a five-minute walk, so he scooped up his bag, complete with packed lunch, a bottle of water and some fruit, and wandered off on his way. His day was just a boring normal school day with George staring out of the window dreaming of the summer holidays that were just around the corner.

The end-of-school bell rang out and almost woke George up! He ran out of the classroom with all his fellow pupils and headed for the school gates. However, to his surprise his grandmother was standing in the playground, talking to the headmaster.

'Gran?' shouted George. 'What are you doing here? And where's Mum?'

His grandmother held out her hands beckoning George to run to her.

George could see a police car up the road. His stomach churned as he asked again, this time in a screech, 'Where's Mum?'

'George, my little man,' said his granny. 'It's all right. Come back with me and I'll explain everything.'

Slowly, and with great care, George's granny explained how his mum and dad had both driven off in his mum's car. The plan was for Mum to drop Dad off at the building society before going to the local shops to pick up food supplies.

The car with Mum and Dad inside was seen leaving the drive. Neighbours saw it turn left at the bottom of the road towards town, CCTV outside the petrol station registered it driving past a few moments later, and that was it! His parents and their car had mysteriously disappeared! No one knows where they went, or why they had not been in contact. The car was not seen on any of the CCTV cameras located further into town. They had completely disappeared, as if they had evaporated into thin air!

Where they went, where they are now, or what has happened to them, no one knows. George doesn't even know if they are still alive, or if something sinister has happened to them.

In his quiet moments, George's mind wanders and dreams up all sorts of fantasies of what has happened and why they can't get in touch with him.

One minute, he is dreaming that they are a pair of secret agents who have gone to save the world like a Mr and Mrs James Bond. Then, he convinces himself they have been abducted by aliens and are flying around the galaxy in a huge spacecraft helping some alien race defend themselves, and they are acting like Captain Kirk and Mr Spock. Or, could a huge hole have opened up and swallowed them up, car and all? And right now, are they driving around in miles of underground tunnels at the centre of the earth, trying to get back home?

That is, when he is in a good mood. On other occasions, George is very sad at the thought that he hasn't seen or heard from either of his parents for almost a year. It's at times like these when he feels alone and very sad. He can't help his thoughts from taking him down into a sad depression.

What if they're dead? he thinks. *What if they were hurt and are in need of help, but no one knows where they are and how to help them?* Sometimes in his dreams he can hear his mother crying out for help, but no one can hear her cries. He wakes up in a cold sweat, his pyjamas and his pillow wringing wet with sweat. He can taste the salty tears that have run down his face while he has been asleep.

A year is a long time for such a young boy. In his despair, he can't help but think that he may never see his parents again. Ever! He can't help his tears.

His pyjamas are all twisted where he has obviously tried to wring them out with his hands during his sleep. His jaw hurts due to the grinding of his teeth, but the worst part is the not knowing, and the feeling of abandonment he feels. His parents are supposed to look after him, not run away and leave him. *How could they be so cruel?* he thinks.

It is when George is at his lowest that his grandmother, aware of what he is going through, always seems to be able to say just the right thing to help soothe his depressive thought pattern and bring him back, at least for a while, into a happier and more relaxed frame of mind.

George moved in with his granny when his parents

disappeared and he has been living with her ever since. No one could believe it. Such a loving family, they would never have just gone off and left their son home alone, but they did. Or at least, that is what the police say happened. There were no signs of a struggle, no ransom note, no letter of explanation, nothing!

All their clothes are still in their wardrobes; their passports are still in the top drawer of Mum's dressing table. No one has tried to remove any money from either of their bank accounts, so how could they have just run away? What are they wearing? How are they supporting themselves? Just as Granny knew her daughter and son-in-law would never leave their son, so George knew his mum and dad would never just go away and leave him. So where are they?

George was slowly growing from a boy into a young man. Little did he know that he was soon to start on his own journey – a journey of exploration into strange new worlds with creatures he could hardly imagine, where all the rules that govern his world just don't exist! But would he, could he, find his parents?

Now the threat of spending the day helping Granny with household chores had been defeated by some quick thinking, George's thoughts returned to the important matter at hand: finishing off his breakfast.

George had his own personal recipe: one third toast, one third butter, and one third homemade marmalade with an extra round of toast on top. Homemade marmalade made by his grandmother! No one could make marmalade and jam like George's granny.

After breakfast, as it was still a little early and George being determined not to get cajoled into doing housework, he decided to take his grandmother's dog Milly for a walk. That was one of the chores George didn't mind doing, as it got him out of the house, and in George's mind, if no one was watching him, it didn't feel like work!

Milly was a rather old golden Labrador, and although she used to love to run in the fields, nowadays she preferred to sit in her favourite chair and watch the birds through the window, dreaming of the days when she would chase them around the garden. She never caught one, not even when she was young and in her prime. They were always far too quick for her, but it never stopped her from trying and she always had that hope that one day she might just catch one.

George put his mug, plate and butter knife into the dishwasher. The dishwasher was another chore he didn't mind doing, as it was simple and so much easier than having to wash up by hand, and Gran didn't let him empty it, as he always put things in the wrong places, so she couldn't find them! Therefore, she thought it easier to empty it herself, but was never quite sure George wasn't just pretending not to know where things went, just to get out of doing it!

Once the pots were done, George ran upstairs to finish getting dressed. As he sat on his bed pulling up his socks, he felt as if something had just moved. He could see something out of the corner of his eye, but when he turned his head there was nothing there. He thought nothing of it. Let's face it, it happens every day. We think we see something or sense movement, but there is nothing there: just a trick of the light, a reflection from a mirror or window, or something moving in the wind. George passed it off and finished putting his socks on.

Once dressed, George ran out of his bedroom and down the stairs three steps at a time, one, two and three

– thud! He had landed at the bottom with so much force, he fell forward and wound up on all fours, just as Granny poked her head around the door.

'George!' she exclaimed. 'How many times have I told you to WALK down the stairs? You'll break your neck one of these days, then where will you be?'

George pondered this for almost a second. *Break my neck and where will I be?* he thought. *I'll be in hospital of course. Why do grown-ups say the most stupid things?*

George thought about all the stories he had heard about how horrible hospital food is, and then he remembered about having to make his bed with hospital corners! *Aargh!!!* he thought. *Hospital certainly isn't for me.*

'Sorry, Gran,' he said. 'I'll take my time in future, I promise.'

He got up nice and slowly.

'Granny!' George shouted. 'Have you seen Milly? I wanted to take her out for a walk but I can't find her.'

'She was under the kitchen table a few minutes ago,' exclaimed Granny, 'hoping to hoover up any breakfast crumbs you may have dropped, but when she realised you weren't likely to drop any food she wandered off, I'm not sure where she is now.'

George was not the athletic sort, although he still had plenty of play-time ahead of him, he liked to sit at home and wait for some news from his parents.

At fourteen years old, slightly over 5 foot 5 inches and 108 pounds, George was typical of the average boy just about to burst into his teens. He had a pale complexion and dark brown hair with slight ginger flecks, almost as if God had given him red highlights. His nose was full of freckles as he had been out in the sun and the other kids at school poked fun at him calling him freckle-face, and some tried to play at joining up the dots on his face, which obviously annoyed him. On many occasions he had tried to wipe all the freckles away, but all he managed to achieve was to give himself a bright-red sore face – something else for the school kids to poke fun at! He spent ages in the shower trying to wash them off. Why did anyone have freckles? What use were they to anyone? Why was life so cruel? *Freckles are stupid*, he thought.

Having been given the brush-off by Milly, George decided to go back into his room to have a look through his computer games. He was going to try to swap some of them with the kids at school. His Gran looked after him as well as she could, but on a widow's pension her funds could not run to all the latest games, so George had to come up with a plan of his own if he wanted to keep up with all the latest ones. Now was as good a time as any to sort them out.

As George sat on his bed, he thought he felt the bed move, as if someone was sitting on it with him. 'Okay, Milly,' he said. 'You didn't want to play when I wanted to, but now you want to play. Well I'm sorry, I have other things to do now. You've missed your chance.'

At this exact moment, George heard the familiar pitter patter of paws as Milly wandered into the room.

'Milly!' George squealed. 'Where have you come from? How did you get off the bed so quickly?' Milly looked at him bemused. She had heard him in his room and wandered in to see if there were any titbits to be had. George often has a stash of biscuits in his room and like most family pets, she knew where a free treat could be found.

As George turned his head away from Milly, he thought he saw a bright yellow scarf – or, at least, half a scarf – disappearing under his bed.

Mice! he thought. *We have mice! No, wait a minute, mice don't wear yellow scarves. In fact, they don't wear any colour scarf, to my knowledge.*

A cat perhaps? So why didn't Milly make a dash for it? I know she is getting a bit old, but surely she wouldn't just sit there and let a cat play in my bedroom without making a fuss, or at least having a bark at it.

George lay face down on his bed and hung his head over the side. He lowered himself slowly over the edge and nervously looked under the bed to see if he could see where the scarf had gone. Slowly, he moved his head, gently, gently, then *whoosh!*, he pulled it up quickly. *Come on, George*, he said to himself. *Don't be silly, there's nothing hiding under the bed. You're fourteen, not four. Don't be a baby!*

Once again, he lowered his head over the side, slowly and with his eyes shut! He opened one eye. Nothing. He opened both eyes, but there was nothing there. A few scraps of biscuit crumbs Milly had missed and a little fluff, but definitely no scarf, yellow or otherwise. He scratched his head and decided he needed a lie down. He had heard grown-ups tell of how tiredness plays tricks on your eyes and he had got up at 8:00 a.m. – not exactly early, but it was for him!

George plumped up his pillow and with a sigh he lay back and closed his eyes.

As his eyes closed, he started to remember a day last summer when he had a real adventure. Well, he *thought* he had an adventure, but to this day he still isn't sure what happened, if anything happened at all. It could have just been a daydream, but if it was, it was the most realistic daydream he had ever had.

George had kept what happened a secret. Mainly

because he was terrified of being made to look a fool, and the truth was so unbelievable even he wasn't sure whether it had actually happened or if he had been hit on the head.

It was a beautiful sunny day in May and he had gone to the village cricket ground with his dad to watch the local team play the team from the next village, Kingsthorpe.

George's dad played, as did most of the older men from the village. George's mum and granny often came and helped the other ladies prepare the tea. The game started around 2.00 p.m., at about 4.00 p.m. they stopped for tea. The home team had the responsibility for making the tea.

This was always the best part for George and the other kids. While the men were talking cricket and eating, and the women were nattering and making tea, and attempting to make it a better tea than the ladies from the other teams! No one was watching the kids and what they ate! So, George and the other children could snaffle far more cake than was good for them, without facing the wrath of their mothers.

When the game finished around 6.00 p.m. to 7.00 p.m., everyone wandered down to the pub, so the men could spend an hour or so drinking beer and reminiscing about the game. Having watched every ball and stroke, George was often surprised by the reminiscing, as it rarely matched the game he had just witnessed! The ball always seemed to be faster or bouncier in the pub talk than it ever was on the pitch, he thought.

The 'game' was supposed to be Twenty-20 cricket, which means each team went into bat and faced 20 overs. An 'over' consisted of six balls being bowled at the opposing team's batsmen, then they changed ends and bowled an over from the other end, then back again and so on. Therefore, a match consisted of each team facing a total of 120 balls. When all 20 overs had been bowled, or if the team were all out before all the balls had been bowled, the other team went into bat and they faced their 20 overs. The winning team was the one with the most runs at the end of the game.

However, there was always another far more important game afoot in English village cricket: at the end of the season, each captain had to send in a nomination from his team to the league's organising committee stating which team had prepared the best tea that season. Obviously, you couldn't vote for your own team.

George liked cricket, but he wasn't quite sure what was the best part of the game – the cricket or the tea! It didn't take him very long to decide that plates full of all sorts of sandwiches, several large home-made cakes, strawberries and cream, washed down with orange juice, lemonade or tea, was the winner!

None of the villagers were any good. If they had been, they would have been poached to play for one of the big-town teams in the district. For the village men, the main idea was to enjoy a fun game on a lovely English Sunday afternoon, a slap-up tea, then a few pints of real ale and a good old blether in the pub afterwards.

The village of Kingsthorpe was a little bigger than George's village, and as such they had a larger population to pick their team from – or that's the reason his dad always gave when they lost to them.

George remembers many summer evenings sitting outside the village pub listening to all the stories about why they had lost that afternoon. He often thought that his dad and the local men had far more fun drinking beer and talking about the game than they ever did actually playing it.

This particular afternoon, George and his dad were walking towards the cricket ground, his dad marching on and George scurrying along behind carrying his dad's cricket bat and pads, daydreaming about how long it would be before he would be old enough to play.

George could hear a car coming up behind them and hoped it was someone who would offer them a lift. It wasn't a long walk, but it wasn't easy for a thirteen-year-old to carry such a big bat and two leg pads! He had quite a shock when a big Land Rover pulled up alongside. The team captain stuck his head out of the car window and spoke to George's dad.

'Hi, Dom,' he said. 'Bad news, I'm afraid. We are going to have to cancel the game today because we can't get a full team. Paul and Harry are still on holiday and Geoff is working, so looks like the game's off.'

'How many players do we have?' asked George's dad.

'We may get to nine if all available people turn up, but that's still two players short,' answered the captain.

'It's a shame, because I quite fancied our chances today and the ladies have already made a lovely tea for everyone. On top of that, the landlord at the local pub will be expecting both teams in for a few drinks around 6.00 p.m., so can you think of anyone we could grab, Dom? They don't have to be any good, all we need is any available bloke to just stand in the outfield right on the boundary to make the numbers up. It seems a shame not to at least have a go, and it's far too early to have tea. It's only 1.00 p.m.'

'I can play! I can play!' shouted George. 'Please, Dad, let me play. And I can get Charlie Elson to play. If we just stand on the outfield, we will both be safe. Please,

Dad, please.'

'I'm not sure, George,' his dad replied. 'The cricket ball is made of hard leather and when they hit it at you it is travelling at quite a speed. If it hit you on the head, it could do you some serious damage.'

'Oh, *please* Dad. If I'm in the outfield, the ball will have slowed down by the time it reaches me. Oh please, Dad, please.'

'Well, I am happy for young George to make his debut, if you feel it's safe,' said the captain. 'And Sid Elson is already at the ground with young Charlie, so I suppose the boys could both make their debut today. It would save us having to cancel, and I certainly don't want to be the one who has to tell the ladies their tea has to go to waste after all the effort they've made. And it would mean they wouldn't be eligible for best tea of the season competition! Do you want to explain that to them, Dom?'

Having to tell fifteen sprightly ladies that they couldn't enter the coveted 'best tea' competition was the clincher for Dominic!

'All right,' said George's dad, 'but you must wear a helmet at all times, George. Okay?'

'Fine, fine,' said George excitedly, 'and thanks, Dad. I'll make you proud, I promise.'

Charlie Elson was George's best friend. They had met on the first day of school seven years ago and had been the best of friends ever since.

Charlie was the same age as George, slightly taller but as skinny as a pole, even though he eats like a horse. The grown-ups say he is growing and needs the food but this annoys George because he eats less and gets told to stop eating or he will get fat! 'Why can Charlie eat what he likes and I can't?' he often complains. 'I'm growing too!'

It was time to start the match. The two team captains tossed a coin to see who went into bat first. 'Heads!' shouted the Kingsthorpe captain, and heads it was.

'We will bat from the pavilion end first,' he gestured, sounding more like Captain Mainwaring from *Dad's Army.*

George and Charlie looked at their captain, awaiting their instructions. They were both hoping to be told 'One of you will bowl first, then the other second', but that was not to be. Instead, they were given the role of fielders, each covering the boundary on opposite sides of the playing field.

'George, you will have the sun in your eyes, so don't take your helmet off, as the peak will protect you from the sun. Charlie, ask your dad to give you his helmet before you go to your position,' ordered George's dad.

Charlie was sent to the far side of the field and George was put right in front of the pavilion. They called it a pavilion, but in reality it was just a wooden hut boarded out on the inside with a couple of pieces of hardboard, so it appeared to be three separate areas.

The middle area was the smallest, with a wooden worktop against the back wall and an old metal sink that the ladies had made into a serviceable little kitchen. They had a trestle table with a large water heater connected to a calor gas bottle. It had to be filled with large bottles of water from the tap, as it wasn't plumbed into the mains water. The hot water was used to make the tea and coffee, and for washing up after the game.

The other two rooms were of a similar size to each other, with old wooden benches and a few old plastic garden chairs. This is where the two teams went to get changed into their cricket whites.

The only light in the pavilion was a glazed window in the kitchen area. Each of the 'changing rooms' had a window-hole cut out of the wooden side wall, with a pair of solid wooden shutters with bolts top and bottom to keep them fastened shut when not in use.

Around the back, they had two tin huts that were used as toilets, although George thinks most of the ladies preferred to walk the short distance back to their homes rather than brave the 'thunder box', as it was called.

About an hour in, and the game was not going to plan. The Kingsthorpe team were knocking the ball all over the pitch and making lots of runs. Charlie had been quite busy on his side of the pitch retrieving the ball and throwing it back to the bowler. Being taller with long arms, Charlie could easily throw the ball the distance required, whereas George, unable to reach the bowler with one throw, would stop the ball and throw it to the nearest member of his own team's fielders, so they could throw it on to the bowler.

Both boys were enjoying themselves. It was a special day to make your debut, and as players they were entitled to first grabs at the best sandwiches. The children had to wait until the players had been fed before they got stuck in!

The sun was beating down and shining right into George's eyes. *If the ball comes high for me to catch it, I won't be able to see it for the sun's glare*, he thought. He was determined to impress his dad and the team captain, as well as to make a bigger mark on the game than Charlie. *Please, please, please hit it towards me, so I can make a catch and be better than Charlie*, he wished, at the same time thinking to himself that Charlie would probably be hoping for the same to happen to him!

George looked around him. His dad's cricket bag was on a bench just twenty feet away, his cricket cap was sticking out from the bag.

The next time the ball gets knocked to the opposite side of the ground, I could nip over there and swap this silly helmet for that cool cap, he thought. *I wouldn't be as hot in Dad's cap. This old helmet is far too hot and sticky. I could see better, and of course I'd look real cool!*

Crack, the sound of willow against leather. The batsman had made a strong contact with the ball, sending it sailing through the air towards the boundary where Charlie was fielding. 'Catch it! Catch it, Charlie!' shouted all the ladies from the pavilion.

'No! Leave it, son,' shouted Charlie's dad. 'It'll break your fingers. Leave it!'

Charlie hadn't heard any of them. He had his mind and his eyes securely fixed on the ball.

This is mine! he thought. *I'll be the hero if I catch this and get their batsman out.*

He moved forward to meet the ball, then checked and moved back, the ball was coming fast and high. *Where is it going to land?* wondered Charlie, *I've got to catch it!*

He moved forward a pace, and then jumped back again, the ball getting closer all the time. Charlie needed to be in the right place to catch it, but it was coming so fast, he couldn't work out if it was going to reach him, or whizz straight over his head. *Oh, where is it going to land? How fast is it coming?* he thought.

Charlie squinted to try to get a better idea of the ball's trajectory, but it was too late: it was right at him, high in the sky and still moving fast. Charlie raised both his hands as high as he could above his head and tried to jump, but it was too late. The ball went between his thumbs, bending them both back, then *bam!*, it landed on the hard ground ten feet from the boundary.

'Hard luck, Charlie!' shouted his Dad and several of his teammates. 'You've saved it going for four. Now throw it back as quick as you can, they're running. Come on, Charlie!'

Charlie picked up the ball. His thumbs were numb with pain from being bent backwards, but he was determined to get the ball back to the bowler to stop Kingsthorpe from making any more runs. He threw it with all his might straight at the wicket.

The Kingsthorpe team were by now a little complacent, with all their runs on the board and knowing the opposition only had 'kids' on the boundary, so the two batsmen were taking it easy and running very slowly between the wickets. As far as they were concerned, the game was already won.

Charlie's throw was perfect, straight at the wicket. With a crack, the ball hit the wicket sending both bails flying high in the air.

'OUT!' shouted Charlie.

'HOW IS HE?!' yelled all his teammates.

The batsman looked at Charlie. While he was wandering back to his crease, the ball had hit his wicket, taken the bails off and he was out, fair and square.

He looked around in disbelief at a beaming Charlie. Although his batting was over for the day, he couldn't help but give Charlie a smile and a pat on the back. 'Well done, lad,' he said. 'That'll teach me not to take anyone for granted. I'll bet we'll be seeing you again next season.'

Charlie was bright red and thought his face was going to split with pride. Although his thumbs were still tingling, it had all been worth it.

Everyone ran towards Charlie and congratulated him.

'Well done, son,' his proud dad exclaimed. 'Your first wicket, well done.'

'Well done, mate,' said George. 'Wow, what a throw... but look at your hands!'

They all looked at Charlie's hands. His thumbs had already started to go a blue colour and had begun to swell up.

'I think your game is over, my boy,' said the captain, 'but well done for the wicket. I'm proud to have you in my team.'

Seeing the move from glorious pride in taking his first wicket to total devastation in being told he was no longer able to play, the captain quickly said to Charlie, 'Perhaps you could go back to the pavilion and help Chris with the scoreboard. We could do with someone like you to make sure he gets it right. We need all the runs we can get.'

A despondent Charlie wandered back to help out with the scoring. He wasn't sure if he should be happy at getting a wicket, or sad to be leaving the game injured, but he knew he had to obey the team captain.

George wandered back with him, his arm over his shoulder. 'Well done, mate. Wow, your first wicket, and against one of the best teams in the league. I can't wait to tell them at school.'

'Thanks,' Charlie replied. 'It's your turn now.'

'I'll do my best,' agreed George, 'but it isn't easy playing in this damn helmet. I can't see a thing in the sun.'

As they reached the pavilion, George looked round to see where his dad was. He was replacing the bails onto the stumps after Charlie's amazing throw and talking to the bowler.

So, while his dad's mind was elsewhere, George

nipped over to his kitbag, whipped off his helmet and grabbed his dad's cap from the bag.

George spun around and was immediately jogging back to his fielding position, just in front of the pavilion, waiting and hoping for a similar ball to come to him, so he could make a catch. *Charlie may have got a wicket, but I could still be the better hero with a clean catch*, he thought.

Ten minutes went by with hardly a ball coming George's way. Then it happened.

Whack! The Kingsthorpe batsman had made a firm strike. The ball rose high in the air and was heading towards the pavilion.

George stared up at the speeding ball. From its height and speed, he estimated it would land about thirty yards to his left, right in the path of where a bunch of ladies from the Kingsthorpe team were sitting chatting and drinking Pimm's with lemonade and eating cake and biscuits.

George had been looking at this particular group for some time, as he was rather hot and always hungry, and although he couldn't have any Pimm's, they also had cool lemonade and food, which he could have!

When he grabbed his dad's cap, he had noticed one of the young ladies putting a small baby into a pushchair after it had gone to sleep in her arms.

Running as fast as he could, George's eyes were darting from the pushchair to the ball and back. He was thinking of what the ball had done to Charlie's thumbs and becoming frightened as to what it could do to the baby if the ball landed in the pushchair, which was now directly in its path.

I won't reach it in time, he thought. *It's travelling far too fast for me to get to it and catch it.*

His eyes fixed on the ball. *If I could only slow it down for a second or two, I may get there in time.*

His mouth was dry and he couldn't speak.

The ladies were enjoying their chatting and hadn't noticed the hard leather ball speeding towards the sleeping baby in the pushchair. The rest of the Kingsthorpe team were in the shade of the pavilion or wandering around the ground, and all of George's team were far too far away on the pitch to be able to do anything. If anyone was going to stop the ball, it had to be George.

He increased his stride, attempting to run even faster towards the pushchair, but he knew the ball was moving much faster than he was capable of running, and he could tell he wasn't going to get to the baby before the ball.

Remembering again the damage the ball had just done to Charlie's hand, he couldn't imagine what it would do if it hit the baby in the face! He stared at the ball spinning through the air.

If only I could move faster, he thought. *If the ball would just slow down, just a little.*

Then he felt his eyes burning as he stared at the ball. His head seemed to get hotter, and he felt his whole body slow down. It was just as if he was wading through treacle.

He was moving, but it was as if in slow motion. However, the rest of the world had stopped completely. All sound had stopped, even the birds in the trees.

Even though he was moving slowly, his cap was slipping off. George grabbed his cap and kept moving as fast as he could.

Panting hard, he continued running towards the sleeping baby. *How is this happening?* he wondered.

Slowly, he pushed his way through the imaginary treacle towards the pushchair. The ball was now only a few feet away, but floating in the air motionless.

I'm not going to make it, thought George. *The baby, the poor baby.*

Then a young girl just appeared out of nowhere! She grabbed the ball as if plucking it from out of the air and held it firm in her hands. She looked straight at George and held the ball out to him.

Still moving slowly through the imaginary treacle, George pushed his way through until he reached the girl. She was standing just inside the cricket boundary, about six feet from the pushchair. He looked at the girl holding out the ball, then *Smack!* The ball was in his hands, the girl had disappeared, and the rest of the world was moving again.

George had caught the ball, partly with his hands and partly with his chest. He held the ball close to his body, and then looked up. Everything was back to normal – sound, motion, everything.

He looked down at the ball nestling in his hands, and then he looked up. His dad was by now running towards him, waving his arms and shouting 'Well done, son!'

The mother of the baby had heard the commotion and realised what had happened. She jumped up. Seeing how close her child had come to being hit by the ball, she ran towards the pushchair and lifted the sleeping baby out. Then she turned towards George and grabbed him and gave him a big kiss, much to his embarrassment.

The lady thanked George for saving her baby from the speeding ball, but appeared totally unaware of how he had moved so quickly and no one mentioned the girl.

By now, most of George's teammates and his dad

had reached him. They all congratulated him and raised his arms in the air as if he were a champion boxer who had just won a prize fight. George stood there in shock.

'Well done, Georgie!' shouted his granny. 'I knew you could make it.'

'Marvelous, my boy!' bellowed his dad. 'Great catch.'

'Well done, mate!' cheered Charlie from the pavilion steps.

All his team congratulated him on the catch, but no one mentioned the stopping of time or the girl. George was both delighted at making a catch and at saving the baby, but he couldn't quite understand what had happened. How come no one else had noticed the girl or the fact he had covered thirty yards in such a short period of time?

If time hadn't stopped and the girl hadn't intervened, I wouldn't have made it to the baby in time, so they all must have noticed, mustn't they? thought George.

The game went on. Kingsthorpe won, but not by the huge margin they had expected to win by, and George and Charlie were heroes for the day. At the end of the game, George wandered about looking for the young girl, but no one had seen her and no one recognised the description. Fearing people would think he had gone mad, or was suffering from sunstroke, he decided to give up his search and get on with eating the sandwiches and cakes instead!

Days passed, weeks passed, then a year, and still no one mentioned the young girl or the fact that George had apparently stopped the ball in mid-air! Eventually, as often happens with the passing of time, George began to think he had imagined the whole thing. After all, no one can appear and disappear into thin air and no one can actually stop time, can they?

So, I must have imagined it, he thought. *I must have been closer to the boundary than I thought, and by looking up in the air as I was running, I had misjudged the distance I had travelled. Yes, that must have been the case. It had been a hot day. The sun must have been playing tricks with my mind. Still, I made the catch, saved the baby, and we all had a great afternoon and a fabulous tea.*

He put the whole idea of stopping time to the back of his mind. After all, what else could he do?

'George! George! Where are you?' shouted his grandmother.

'Wha—? Who? What?' murmoured George still coming round from his slumber. 'What's the matter, Gran?' he asked.

'George Thomson, why are you lounging in bed at 10:00 o'clock on such a beautiful morning?' she replied in a gruff tone. 'Don't you have better things to do? If not, I am sure I can find you something. There are always chores to be found for lazybones.'

In great fear of being given a very long list of chores, George jumped up in a flash, kissed his gran on the cheek and was soon out of his room, down the stairs three-at-a-time again, and in the kitchen searching for his mobile phone. He never left the house without his phone: what if his Mum and Dad called while he was out?

Wiping his brow, he pulled on his shoes and ran around to his best friend Charlie's house.

George told Charlie all about the scarf and the bump on his bed that he thought was Milly.

'Well, it *could* have been Milly jumping off the bed,' suggested Charlie, 'and as for the half a scarf, I think you must have imagined it. Anyway, you don't have a yellow scarf, and where did it go? Scarves don't just appear from nowhere and then vanish into thin air. I suggest you don't tell anyone about this, mate, or they will put you away in the nuthouse. People seeing vanishing scarves in their bedroom – a definite case for the funny farm, if you ask me.'

With the conversation over, George and Charlie wandered off to play in the lanes and fields around the village. They lived in Alden on the Staffordshire–Derbyshire border in the heart of the English countryside. It was a very quiet little village about a forty-minute drive from Birmingham, thirty-five minutes from Nottingham and Leicester, and fifteen minutes from Derby. London was just over an hour by train, which made Alden a great place for parents to commute from, but a bit quiet for a couple of fourteen-year-old boys to grow up in.

No cinema, no fast-food restaurants, no bowling alley, no football team to watch on a Saturday afternoon. The village did have a local Sunday football league team, but they played on Sunday mornings while George and his grandmother were at church.

Given the choice, he would have preferred to be watching football, but he was never given the option. Church was important to his grandmother, and his grandmother was important to George.

After a couple of hours playing in the fields, skimming stones over the river and climbing trees, the boys decided it was time for lunch. Like most fourteen-year-old boys, they were ruled by their stomachs. George was a good boy and generally did as he was told, so his grandmother was happy for him to play out as long as he kept in touch and was never late for meals.

After almost a full second of deliberation, the boys

decided they would both go to Charlie's house to eat. As soon as they arrived, George phoned his gran to tell her he was staying there for lunch and to check if there had been any word from his mum and dad. He tried not to use his mobile phone if he could help it, as he didn't like paying the bill and he wanted to save his battery. Imagine if his mum and dad were trying to call him and he missed the call because he had a flat battery! The thought turned his blood cold!

His gran was a great cook and could make some wonderful tasty meals out of almost anything, even when there appeared to be nothing in the larder. But with his granny's food everything was 'good for you' and felt like it would stick to your insides for ever.

On the other hand, Charlie's mum made pizza and burgers and things George's gran thought of as new-fangled or foreign, or not good for you. So, lunch at his best friend's house was always a treat for George.

Charlie's Mum greeted them with a smile and asked, 'What's it to be, boys? Pizza, burger, fish fingers, or shall I pop some sausages in the oven? I could rustle up a nice plate of sausage, egg and beans if you fancy it.'

Sausages were a particular favourite of both boys, so the deal was struck.

Sausage, egg, beans and thick crusty bread with real butter. What a treat for two young intrepid adventurers! However, what our two young adventurers didn't know was that poached eggs, beans and wholemeal bread are good for you, and the sausages were quorn instead of meat, and when roasted in the oven instead of fried are also rather good for you. So, they were sort of eating healthily and didn't even know it.

Like many mums, Charlie's mum knew children hated the idea of health foods, but she had learnt how to make the boys eat their meals by making them appear to be fast food or unhealthy whilst actually being full of goodness. As they say, mums know best!

CHAPTER 2

George meets Leonard

After a feast of sausages, with not a mention of salad or anything good for you, George and Charlie ventured out for the afternoon's activities with full stomachs.

One of their favourite places was the river. The boys liked to sit on the bridge and dangle their feet over the wall. The river was really just a little stream, hardly any fish in it but nevertheless a great place to play pirates or battleships, and over the years the two boys had enjoyed many an adventure at this spot.

Charlie decided to run and fetch some sticks to throw in the water – they liked to see which would float and bet on which one would appear under the bridge first. Then, they would throw stones at the sticks to try to sink them. They knew watching sticks floating under a bridge was something Winnie the Pooh did, and at fourteen years old they were not exactly happy with the thought of playing at Winnie the Pooh, so the stone-throwing made them feel they were doing something more like older tough boys would, as Winnie the Pooh would never throw stones.

George sensed Charlie approaching, so he turned to get his supply of sticks, but Charlie wasn't there. He turned back to see him about fifty yards away collecting sticks. There was a crack and George spun round. 'Who's there?' he said. No one replied.

He was just about to shout to Charlie when a bright yellow scarf drifted long in the water from under the bridge. He reached in and pulled it out. It was bone dry!

How could it be dry if it was in the water? He threw it back in the water to see if it got wet, but it vanished.

Just then, Charlie appeared with an armful of sticks.

'What's up, mate?' he said. 'You look like you've seen a ghost.'

George explained what had happened. Charlie was his best friend and George was not one for telling tales. However, Charlie was now beginning to get a little fed up of the vanishing scarf game and told George to stop going on about things that obviously are not there, as it was starting to be annoying – and spooky!

'I'm telling you, mate, they will lock you up and throw away the key if you aren't careful,' mocked Charlie.

'I know,' George replied, 'but I tell you I saw the scarf. I picked it up and it wasn't wet.'

'Okay, if you are going to go on and on about it, I'm going home.'

Charlie turned and walked away.

'Don't go!' George shouted, looking up. 'I promise I won't mention it again.'

His friend stopped and turned around.

'All right, but this is your final chance. One more daft ghost story and I'm off.'

The boys wandered down the lane and climbed over a gate into one of the big open fields. They often took this route back home, as it was quite a lot shorter than walking all the way around the field. The only problem was that the farmer who owned the field didn't take kindly to having people wandering about on his land. However, if they kept their eyes open, they could usually get across without anyone seeing them.

As they got roughly into the middle of the field they were confronted by a very large and obviously very old oak tree. George didn't want to say anything, in case he made Charlie angry again with a ghostly tree remark, but he was convinced he had never noticed the tree right in the middle of the field before. His head said *Say nothing!* but his mouth just came blurting out with it: 'Charlie, can you see that tree?'

'Of course I can,' Charlie snapped. 'I'm not the one seeing things that aren't real, you know.'

He pushed the sole of his shoe against the base of the huge tree. 'See, it's solid, it's real!'

'Okay, but have you seen it before?' asked George.

Charlie stopped and looked at what to him was a normal - if a somewhat large - oak tree, the kind you see everywhere in the English countryside. Then he thought again. 'Hmm, now you come to mention it, no I haven't. Maybe it's new?'

'Don't be silly,' laughed George. 'It takes hundreds of years for a tree to grow like that. Wait a minute, is that a door in the side of the trunk?'

'A door in a tree? Does it have a yellow scarf as a handle?' mocked Charlie.

Both boys looked around to see if they could see any other new trees, but the rest of the landscape looked normal. When they turned back the oak tree had gone!

'What happened?!' shouted George. 'Where's the tree gone?'

Charlie sat down hard on the ground. 'I dunno mate. It was there, then it wasn't!'

'Could we both be seeing things now?' asked George. 'Now do you believe me about the yellow scarf?'

'A tree isn't a scarf,' replied Charlie.

'No, but we both saw something that wasn't there, didn't we, and anyway a tree that big couldn't fit under my bed! The scarf appeared and then disappeared, and now a huge tree has appeared and disappeared, only this time you saw the tree as well.'

'I suppose so,' quipped Charlie. 'What do you think it means? Are we both going mad? I don't think we should tell anyone. I don't want to end up in the funny farm – they have really bad food there!'

That was enough for George. He could cope with many things but bad food wasn't one of them.

Charlie thought for a minute. 'Do you think someone is playing a game with us?' he asked.

'Why would they do that, and how did they make a tree appear and disappear? That's some trick!' exclaimed George.

'Okay, George. 'So what just happened then?' asked Charlie. 'Is it a message? If so, what's the message and who is sending it? Is it a warning? If so, what is it telling us? What sort of message is a tree appearing and disappearing? Is the world about to be bombarded by huge oak trees? And anyway, who is trying to send us a message?'

George thought long and hard.

'A message? Could it be from my parents? Are they telling me where they are?'

'What do you mean?' said Charlie. 'Do you think they are living up an oak tree wearing a yellow scarf?'

'Don't be stupid,' snapped George. 'My parents do not live in a tree!'

'Well, what are you saying then? What's the message, and who is it from?' asked Charlie.

He reached into his pocket and took out his iPhone. His parents were a little richer than George's grandma and could afford to give him an iPhone instead of a simple mobile phone. Charlie typed in 'oak tree' and 'yellow sca'. The internet didn't need any more. It came back with 'Tie a Yellow Ribbon Round the Ole Oak Tree', a song released in 1973 by Tony Orlando & Dawn.

'That's it!' shouted George, peering at Charlie's phone over his shoulder. 'How could I be so stupid? It wasn't half a scarf, it was a ribbon! That song was one of my parents' favourite songs. They used to sing it to me when I was a baby. They must be alive and are trying to make contact with me!'

'Through a tree?' smirked Charlie 'How will that work? I still think you're going mad and it looks like I'm going mad too. It must be the sausages, I thought they tasted funny!'

'Don't be daft,' George replied in a fluster. 'Mum and Dad are out there and they will come and get me, just you see.'

'Hmm,' said Charlie, 'I don't know. I thought I saw a tree, but now it isn't there. I think the heat is getting to me and all I need is a drink of water and a small lie-down. It was those sausages, perhaps they were off, or something. They're giving us both hallucinations, mate.

'I'm off home to watch the TV and see if I can find some ice cream in the freezer, and I think you should do the same, George. Please let me know if you have a flying saucer landing in your bedroom,' he mocked.

George looked at Charlie. He didn't know what to say. Nothing made sense. The scarf, the tree, nothing. The boys looked again at the spot where the tree had appeared, gave each other a 'high five', then ran off back to the village and their homes. Charlie went home to watch TV and eat ice cream while George went and sat on his bed to try to make some sense of the day.

He wanted to tell his gran what had been happening, but as he didn't know the answers yet, he thought he should keep it quiet until he knew what was going on.

After all, he didn't want to upset his gran. She was his mother's mother and was probably missing her as much as he was, so he didn't want to give her any false hope.

His gran had been his entire world since the disappearance of his parents. She was obviously as worried as George but had never shown her true feelings. At first, he thought she knew where they were and what was going on. If she didn't, surely she would be more concerned. Then, he thought she was just being brave to make him feel better. It was bad enough him feeling as he did without his gran falling apart as well. So, he convinced himself that his gran was playing the part of the perfect adult and keeping her feelings in check for his sake. Grown-ups did that sort of thing, he mused.

As he sat there, the hairs on the back of his neck started to tingle and he suddenly felt a chill. He knew something was wrong but he didn't know what. All seemed normal, but his tingling neck had him worried.

He looked down at the bottom of his bed to the place where he thought Milly had been sitting earlier and there it was! The yellow ribbon. This time, it had some writing on it: **Jackson. Five. Pond. Tree.**

What did it mean? George thought hard, he didn't know if he should run around to Charlie's house or shout his gran. What was he to do?

The Jackson Five, that was the name of the pop group with Michael Jackson and his brothers. **Five** and **Pond** could mean five pounds. So, should he spend £5 on a Jackson Five CD? But how on earth could buying a pop CD from the '70s help bring his mum and dad back?

This was crazy and the more George thought about it, the sillier it became. The song about the yellow ribbon was a '70s song. George knew that much, but he couldn't remember who the singer was and he was sure it was far too naff to be a Michael Jackson song. He racked his brains and then he remembered what Charlie's iPhone had told them. The song had something to do with Orlando, and his mum and dad had been there on holiday the year before he was born, so it had sentimental memories for them.

WAIT A MINUTE!!! Had his mum and dad been at Disney World all this time, on HOLIDAY?

George was shaking, then he took a few deep breaths to help him to calm down.

Come on George, think! he said to himself.

Then he remembered, the police had found both his parents' passports in the top drawer of their dressing table and if they had gone on holiday to Disney World, they would certainly have needed to take their passports with them.

And what about his gran? She didn't know where they were, and if they had gone on holiday, they would have told Granny. No, there had to be another explanation – but what?

Then George remembered something his granny often told him: If you have a problem, no matter what it is, your brain will figure it out if you give it time. In real life, things do not always just pop into your mind like they do in the TV detective stories. Sometimes, you just need to let a problem run about in your mind and eventually the answer will come to you. Gran said your brain is like a big cupboard full of all the things that have happened to you and you just need time for your brain to have a rummage through everything, so it can find the answers you are looking for. A bit like finding a matching pair of socks in George's sock drawer. If you rummage around long enough, you'll find a matching pair!

That is all well and good if you have plenty of time,

but George wanted the answer now. It would soon be 5.00 p.m. and Granny would be calling him in for tea. How was he going to save his parents before teatime when he hadn't a clue what was going on? *Oh, if only Dad were here to help*, thought George.

Then it came to him, just like Granny said it would. On the outskirts of the village there is a dog-walking area called Jackson's Hollow, and in the middle is a pond with a large oak tree growing on the edge. George and Milly used to play there when she was a pup. George was always getting into trouble for letting her swim in the water and returning her home filthy and wet, but how was he supposed to keep a puppy from jumping into the water?

George looked back at the writing on the ribbon. It was 4:50 p.m. Could the **Five** mean 5.00 p.m.? If so, he had ten minutes to get there, and that would require a very quick run as Jackson's Hollow was at the far side of the village. George grabbed his phone, pulled on his trainers and ran for all he was worth.

The church clock was striking five when George arrived at the spot. There was no one about, and even though it was a beautiful sunny day the area felt dark and damp. George wasn't frightened: this was a message from his parents and they would never hurt him. But what if the message wasn't from his parents? What if it was from the people who abducted his parents and now they were coming back for him?

George was bent forward with his hands on his knees, he was puffing and panting after his run. He had a lump in his throat as he stared at the old oak tree. Goose pimples were popping up on his skin and he was sure the temperature had dropped a few degrees. A strange, sweet smell filled the air and he could see a little mist like a five-foot-long cloud gathering at the side of the tree.

George stared at the little cloud. It started off almost clear, then it grew darker and denser until he could no longer see through it. Then, with a squeak, it changed colour to a bright pink and a little door appeared to open in its side.

George was both petrified and excited at the same time. He couldn't move a muscle or utter a word, then he saw a foot appear out of the little door and a small man climbed out. He was wearing a full three-piece suit in burgundy with a brilliant white shirt and a burgundy bow tie. He had a fob watch hanging off his waistcoat and a cane in his hand. He was no more than three feet tall and very old – well, he was to George. He was sixty if he was a day!

'Hello,' he said. 'My name is Leonard. Pleased to meet you at last. I've heard a lot about you. Oh, and well done for working out my clues. Your Dad has always said you were a clever boy and could work things out. Have you ever heard that song about the yellow ribbon? Absolutely awful! Why they picked that one I will never know. Prefer a bit of the Rambling Stones or Ernest Priestley myself.'

Ernest Priestley? thought George.

'That's *Presley*,' said George, 'Elvis Presley. And it's the *Rolling* Stones, not Rambling Stones, even I know that.'

George stared at the funny little man, not quite sure if he was seeing things. 'Who are you? Do you know my parents? Have they sent you to get me? Where are my mum and dad? Why have you come...'

Leonard butted in. 'All in good time, my boy. All in good time.'

CHAPTER 3

The Quest Begins

George continued to stare at Leonard. He felt rooted to the spot, his mouth was dry and he could feel the blood rushing through his body. Bowing his head, he stared at his feet and took deep breaths, then the words started to come back to him.

'Who? Where? What?' he mumbled.

'My name is Leonard, pronounced *Lenard*,' said the little man. 'I have many names, but this one will suffice for a human child from your time. There are many things you need to know, and I'm sure you have many questions. However, we must start at the beginning.'

Leonard took a deep breath and began to speak, waving his cane in the air as he did so.

'I am many thousands of your years old and I am from a different time and place. They call me a "Keeper". I don't really know why, because I don't actually keep anything. I would prefer "Searcher" or just Leonard, however they named my kind centuries ago, so I suppose it is far too late to change it now. Anyway, I am sure you have far more interesting things to ask me, and I can't be seen here in this form talking to you, so grab my hand and jump up on my cloud.'

'But I'll fall through a cloud,' squeaked George, his mind still confused at what he was experiencing.

'Not this one you won't,' responded Leonard. 'This is my home, my means of transport, my everything really. It only looks like a cloud when I am on earth. When I am on other worlds, it looks like other simple local objects that blend in with the background. Fancy trying to look like a cloud on Paragus 3, it would stand out like a sore thumb, or even worse on Dius Major, that would be a sight to see! Anyway, grab my hand and climb aboard, young George.'

George was totally bemused and still a little frightened, but the little man seemed friendly and he said he knew where his mum and dad were, so he decided it was safe enough to do as Leonard said, at least for now.

George took Leonard by the hand and climbed up onto the cloud. It felt hard but soft at the same time, and George could smell a fragrant smell like fresh flowers.

'Make yourself at home, young George,' said Leonard. 'Try that chair for size – your father loved that chair.'

George looked around him. The internal space was considerably bigger than it looked outside.

Leonard started to explain: 'That was because the cloud you saw outside was just the illusion I had made, and if you had been able to see it as it really was, you would have noticed it was much bigger. Having said that, I can make it bigger and smaller if I wish. Sometimes I am alone and don't need space, and sometimes I have to carry many people, creatures or objects, so it helps if I can expand and decrease the size to suit my needs or mood. I sometimes make it bright and sometimes dark, it all depends on how I'm feeling. I like change, do you?'

At this point Leonard looked down at his burgundy suit and blinked. It changed into a bright blue colour with matching bow tie.

'How did you do that?' said George.

'As I said, I change things to suit my mood and now I've found you I feel happy. Bright blue is my happy colour,' replied Leonard with a smile.

'So where are my parents? When can I see them?' cried George.

'Well now, that is the question,' Leonard said mysteriously. 'That is the reason I have come back to get you, because we have...' he paused '...lost them!'

'What?!' shouted George. 'First you tell me my parents have sent you to get me, and now you tell me you have lost them! How can you lose two fully grown people?'

'Well YOU did!' countered Leonard, clearly in a huff about being blamed for Dominic and Lucy's disappearance. 'So don't you blame me!'

He turned his face away, folded his arms and looked up at the ceiling to show that he felt rather hurt by George's comments.

'I didn't LOSE them! They WENT AWAY,' George sobbed.

Leonard puffed out his cheeks.

'Well then, they have "gone away" again, haven't they? Only this time, I think I can explain where they went. Well, sort of.'

'Look,' said George, in a demanding tone. 'I think you had better sit down and tell me what is going on, and while you are at it we need to let my grandmother know where we are. Well, at least, where *I* am!'

'Hmm,' mused Leonard. 'I suppose you're right, but don't worry about your grandmother. We will return soon, and when we do it will be to 5.00 p.m. on the same day, so she will never have missed you.'

'But it is already ten past five,' argued George, 'so how can we come back at 5.00 p.m.? That's impossible.'

'Well, not actually. It may appear to you and your kind to be impossible, but I do it all the time. I keep track of all the people who move about in time and space.

45

That is what I do: I keep things where they should be.'

'So that must be why they call you a "Keeper" then,' observed George. 'Because you KEEP track of people. And of things!'

'Oh, I suppose I do. I hadn't thought of it like that! Your dad was right, you are a bright boy,' remarked Leonard. 'A bright boy indeed.'

'So how come you haven't kept track of my mum and dad? Where are they? And when are they?'

That bit just didn't sound right to George. *When* are they? But he had been told things were different in Leonard's world and he was just going with the flow.

'I think you have some explaining to do and if you don't want to feel the hard end of my granny's rolling pin, I suggest you start talking,' demanded George.

'I tell you what, why don't we go back to your grandmother's house and I will tell you both all about it. It's coming up to teatime and your mum and dad have told me many times about your gran's stew and dumplings. I've never actually tasted a dumpling, so how about it?' suggested Leonard.

George thought this was a great idea. He wasn't frightened exactly, but he was a little concerned, and he knew when he got back home his grandmother would know what to do.

Leonard blinked his eyes again, and in a flash he and George were sitting in Grandma's kitchen. The smell of stew and dumplings filled the room.

'You're just in time, George... and who is this?' asked Grandma. 'And why is he so little?'

'Gran, I am SOOO pleased to see you. Hang on—' said George, looking straight at Leonard. 'How did you know we were having stew and dumplings for tea? I didn't know what was for tea.'

Leonard smiled and shrugged his shoulders. 'I came here earlier and saw them,' he said. There are still many things you don't know about me and where I come from, but there is plenty of time. Let's eat and I will explain.'

George looked up at his grandma and tried to tell her about the tree and the yellow scarf that turned out to be a ribbon, and Leonard climbing out of the cloud with tales of being sent by his mum and dad, but all his words came out far too fast and all jumbled.

Granny just smiled. She appeared to understand what George was trying to explain, sometimes even before he got the words out.

George didn't know what to expect from his grandma. He knew his story would sound unbelievable, but it was true and he had always been told to tell the truth, and anyway, he had Leonard there with him to prove it. But would Granny believe a three-foot-tall man in a bright-blue suit?

He looked over to where she was sitting and then back at Leonard. They were both looking at each other with smiles on their faces. George slumped in his chair, his story told and his part done. Now it was up to Granny to have her say and he wasn't quite sure what response he was going to get. The times Granny had instilled in him not to play with strangers – and they didn't come much stranger than Leonard! What was his granny going to do?

'Right,' said Grandma. 'So, now you are calling yourself Leonard. You have put on a little weight around the middle but lost some height since I last saw you.'

She smiled and looked straight at Leonard. There was a big grin all over Leonard's face.

'Yes, my sweet girl, I have changed a little,' he replied with a smile.

'*Sweet girl?*' giggled George. 'This is my grandmother and she hasn't been a girl for over fifty years!'

'George!' snapped Granny. 'Don't be rude. When I last saw Leonard, he was a tall, slim gentleman with thick black hair and a beautiful smile. I was just a young girl at the time. We had a few adventures together in the summer of 1969. The Americans had just put a man on the moon and it had made a few changes in the way things were.'

'Yes, the moon landing wasn't supposed to happen quite so soon, so I was sent to "put things right". I needed some help and your grandmother was the one I chose to help me in my quest.'

'WHAT?!' exclaimed George. 'Granny helped the Americans reach the moon? My granny? But why Granny? Why my mum and dad? Why me?'

'No, no,' Leonard reassured him. 'Your granny didn't help the Americans. She helped me sort out the mess that came afterwards.'

'I still don't understand,' said George, feeling quite lost for words now.

'It's quite simple, my little man,' explained Leonard. 'You see, your world is made up of many people, around seven billion at the last count. You explained it quite well earlier. Most of your people see nothing and sense nothing, they just go about their business on autopilot, unaware of the little changes going on around them.

'Then there are some more sensitive souls who think they see things out of the corner of their eye, a change in temperature, a different smell, or sense some kind of presence. Of course, when they have a look, they see nothing. So they put it down to tiredness or their imagination.

'And then there are the gifted ones, people who are

sure they have seen something, but are never required by the Creator to enter our realm. So their potential is never fulfilled.

'And finally, there are the special ones. Human souls that are blessed with the ability to actually see and travel into other dimensions, into other worlds.'

'What?!' shouted George. 'You mean like spacemen? And who is the Creator?'

'Not really.' Interjected Leonard. 'Let me explain. You see, when you think you see or feel something that you cannot explain, when you get the sensation that you are not alone, well the chances are that it is a Keeper, just like me, passing by as they are travelling between worlds. We have doors and tunnels that connect the worlds together like a giant invisible spider's web, all connected, but unseen by the general population of most worlds.

Think of a tennis ball with a drinking straw sticking out of it. Now attach another ball to the other end of the straw. A small creature in the first ball could now walk along the inside of the straw and go from one ball to the other and back again using the straw as a tunnel.

'Now think of thousands and thousands of balls the size of your planet Earth, all attached by invisible tunnels that only special people can see and move around in.

'When we are moving from one world or place to another, we sometimes have to pop up into a place to get our bearings.

'We can look just like a human on earth, or a Bragadon from Dius Major, a plant or a bird, a living thing or an inanimate object. It doesn't matter where we are, we can always blend in. We have to, or the local people would know we were not of their kind, and that would never do, would it?

'Plants, inanimate objects or animals are easy,' Leonard continued. 'It's you humans that cause me the most trouble when trying to blend in. One of my hardest tasks is keeping up with your fashion here on earth! Why do you have to change your clothes and hair so often? Popping up in 2020 wearing a fashion from 1920 causes such problems for me.'

'But how many worlds are there?' asked George.

'I don't think anyone really knows,' replied Leonard. 'The Creator is still making new worlds as we speak, while some others are dismantled and reborn, usually because some inhabitants have evolved and caused so much harm to their natural habitat that the only way of resolving the issue is to dismantle their world and start again.

'Therefore, at any time there are probably billions of worlds, all in various stages of evolution. I have been to many thousands and that is just the tip of the iceberg, so to speak. Think of it as pages in a very large book. Your world could be page number 1,000 in a book of 50,000 pages. So there are 999 other worlds in front of your world and 49,000 worlds behind it. There are also many other books, just like in a library. However, the books and the pages are not fixed in any way, so they often all change places, like someone ripping a page out of one book and putting it back somewhere else. If you didn't read every book, you wouldn't know a page had moved, but if you tried reading a book with a wrong page in a critical part of the story, then the story wouldn't make sense would it?'

George could feel his head spinning.

Leonard continued: 'The people in your book – sorry, in your *world* – think this is the only world, and are blissfully unaware of what is going on in all the other worlds. It is my job to try to keep it that way. To keep all of the books and all of their pages in the right order. I have to keep track of things and put back any pages that fall into the wrong place. It is sometimes very hard to remember which world is which, and who is who, and what should be happening. If I get confused, I can call on a Master Keeper to show me the path things should be moving along, its then up to me to do all I can to make this happen as it is supposed to.'

'Let me get this straight: there are thousands and thousands of Georges, and thousands and thousands of Grannies?' said George.

'Well, yes,' replied Leonard. 'But not all worlds are the same, and they are not all inhabited by *Homo sapiens.* It's not usual for the Creator to mix species from different worlds. There are plenty of worlds for your species to move around on without causing even more problems by sending you to worlds with different atmospheres or water-breathing species.

'On some of the other worlds where your species have evolved, the First World War never happened, and in some worlds, mankind is still living in caves trying to master fire. In other worlds, mankind is far more advanced, they have already invented— I shouldn't say any more in case I give you ideas you are not yet ready to understand. But you get the picture, I hope.'

'There is one Creator who has made all the worlds, all the land, mountains, skies and water. He gives life to spirits, or souls as I believe you call them on your world. Each soul is given an earthly body to inhabit for its "mortal life" on a world. When its earthbound life ends and the physical body dies, the soul returns to the Creator to see what it has learned from its earthly life.

'The Creator could have made all souls in his own image and with a perfect mix of compassion, love, faith, etc, but he felt that by doing so he would have created robotic beings with no real understanding of what love is, or compassion, or any other true feelings, or emotions, good or bad. Therefore, he decided to give all souls a free will. His plan is for every soul to live out their lives, so they can work out for themselves the true meaning of life, love, peace and freedom by making their own mistakes and learning from them by feeling, experiencing and living a real and fulfilled life!'

'If he had not done this, you would all be nothing more than robots with no free thought. You would all do as you were told, just like a computer. You would do what the Creator implanted into your head at birth and you would not be able to think for yourself.

'Obviously, it takes time for everyone to learn all the lessons they need to know – it can take many of your earth lifetimes for some people. Some people are a little slow to learn, while others get it much quicker. Eventually, all mankind will have lived long enough to have made all the mistakes, learned valuable lessons from them, and so grown into the serene beings the Creator always wanted them to be. But each soul must do it for themselves by feeling their mistakes through living and learning, just like a human baby learns. You're not born knowing fire will hurt you, but it is needed for keeping you warm and to cook your food. So, you all learn as you live. Your world is your classroom for you to live and learn through life experience.

'When a spirit is on your world and is living a "free life" as you know it, then it has the free will to do as it wishes. However, because the reason a spirit is living on any world is to learn lessons from experience, if a spirit does bad things in life, it will be taught the error of its ways either here on earth, or when it returns to the

Creator's classroom after its body dies. The thing that connects all worlds is the spirit or soul of its living creatures.'

'What do you mean "after it dies"?' exclaimed George. 'Are you saying my mum and dad are dead?'

A tear came into his eyes.

'No, no,' Leonard quickly replied 'They are still very much alive.'

George gave out a little gasp of relief. He couldn't help a small tear rolling down his face.

'But how do you know they're alive, if you don't know where they are?' asked George.

'As I said, I'm a Keeper. I am not human as you understand the term. I told you about the special people who can see and sense things but don't know what they are experiencing. Well, on some worlds there are a few chosen people with the ability to move between worlds. We call these people "Day-Trippers". They can move about from world to world during their lives, but only occasionally, and they must eventually return to live out their original life on their original world. They are human as you understand the term.

'Therefore, if a Keeper like me needs a little help to put something right, he searches out a Day-Tripper to help him, or her. It is very rare, but sometimes a Day-Tripper proves themselves to be a worthy soul and so they evolve into a Keeper and continue with our quest. Keepers can also evolve over time into Master Keepers.

'A Master Keeper is like a teacher. They teach the truth, and their role is to teach all souls how to find the right way to interpret the true meaning of their lessons through their own understanding of life. So eventually we can eradicate all bad things from all worlds. It is imperative that all humans find the truth and the right way for themselves. It is wrong to dictate to anyone, even when you are telling them about lessons – even very important lessons.

'The correct way is to let them find the way for themselves, so they join the dots themselves and remember the lessons and why they have come to the conclusion as to what is right and what is wrong, and why it is so. As there are plenty of bad people in most worlds, the teachers have their work cut out.

'One day, probably billions of your earthly years from now, all worlds will be harmonious and will have eradicated suffering, famine, war and hardship for themselves. When this has taken place, the role of the Masters and teachers will have been completed and all living creatures will have learnt to live together in a state of total peace and harmony. Until then, our work goes on.

'Master Keepers usually stay away from the day-to-day life of living spirits like yourself. It's our job as Keepers to help Master Keepers by being amongst the spirits in their human form and keep our eye out for any Day-Trippers that look like they are turning bad, and causing potential mass harm by using their Day-Tripper powers to upset the natural path on other worlds.

'All people in your world and all the other worlds have one thing in common: you all have an inner spirit. This is made up of your brain and your heart, and it travels with you wherever you go.'

'Wherever we go?' said George. 'Even when we die?'

'Sort of. It is death, but death isn't what you think it is. However, if all of mankind knew what awaited them at the end of their mortal life on earth, then their life would have a completely different meaning. It is obviously important therefore that we keep ourselves and the truth a secret until the end of the mortal life.

'Consider for a moment that you have been put here on earth to live out your life and learn from your experiences so you can evolve into an enlightened being. However, if you knew how you were going to die, when you were going to die and what happens after your death, then how could you possibly live a normal life? You could avoid the day of your death, thus causing considerable change to the master plan. You could lead pointless lives without the ability to learn if you have nothing to fear from death as you now know it. You may as well be just an android or a computer with no feelings, and that was what the Creator wanted to avoid in the first place.

'The way things are now, when you "die" as you know it, you can go back to one of the Creator's classrooms to review what you did during the life. The teacher can go through what you have learnt with you and send you back to earth at a different time, in the right place and in the right life to learn the specific lessons you still need to learn.

'For example, if you hurt animals when you are alive, you may be returned for a short time as an animal, so you can feel for yourself what it is like. That would be a valuable lesson learnt. If you do something to another person, you can come back and have that happen to you, again a good lesson learnt. I have heard it called "karma" on your world.

'However – and this is why I am here – many years ago, something went wrong. A Day-Tripper was involved with a very bad person and the fun and excitement he felt from doing the bad deeds made him decide to continue with the bad ways. He found that he was actually enjoying the chaos, pain and death that came about because of his deeds. He became so bad and twisted from the mayhem and suffering his actions caused that we had to do something to stop him.'

'But' interjected George. 'If the Creator is so all-powerful, why didn't the Creator just stop him?'

Leonard smiled, and continued. 'The Creator allows this to happen, to a degree. It's all about allowing you to express free will again. However, the Creator put in a failsafe to protect the worlds from long-term chaos by giving you humans such short mortal lives. He thought there would be a limit to the evil anyone can do in your earthly lifespan and if someone did look like they were causing too much trouble, then he could arrange for the bad person to be returned earlier.

'No matter how bad a spirit turns, its body will eventually die and then the soul will be returned to the Creator's classroom to look back at their actions and be nurtured and taught the true path to long-lasting peace.'

'Okay,' began George, 'I think I'm getting the basic idea, but how can anyone work against such a powerful Creator?'

Leonard continued: 'The free spirit the Creator gave to every soul comes with a vast responsibility, and some spirits are not up to the task of taking responsibility for their own lives – well, not until they have had a few lessons. On top of that, some of your governments remove the freedom of individuals so they don't feel responsible for their own actions. The "nanny state" I believe you humans call it.

'This gives birth to spirits that want to fight against authority, which in some situations is a good thing, but it can also force otherwise decent spirits to start along the wrong path towards the evil side of life. Fighting oppression and evil is fine, until the freedom fighters lose sight of their true goals. The oppressed can then become the aggressors and the whole battle starts all over again.

'Not everything is down to evil doings. Sometimes, things just go wrong or happen in the wrong time, like the man on the moon in 1969! It wasn't supposed to happen until 1977, and sometimes the bad people take advantage of the situation and make things go wrong, or try to change things for their benefit. The bad spirits brought the moon landing forward hoping to cause World War III between Russia and America, but we were able to jump in at the last minute and stop it. That caused quite a stir I can tell you, as I'm sure you would imagine.

'There was a lot of midnight oil burnt during that time, but we managed to prevent the war, even though we couldn't stop the early moon landing. So now, in your world, 1969 goes down in history as the first moon landing and there never was a World War III – well, not yet anyway!'

'What?!' shouted George.

'Calm down,' insisted Granny. 'Let Leonard finish, George.'

'Thank you, Elizabeth, I will continue. The gift of day-tripping usually gets passed down in the genes. This is because the valuable lessons your spirit has learned are stored in the DNA, and the soul of the newborn baby. It can access them as and when they are needed, if the mind is educated and is in tune with its soul.

'Your Grandmother has the ability to be a Day-Tripper, as does your mother, and yes, so do you. It is unusual for any one world to have more than a few Day-Trippers living at any one time. As you mortal earthlings only live for such short lifetimes and are so easily damaged, it is often the case that some get killed before they ever know they have the power.

'Sometimes a bad spirit can sense that a child is going to turn into a Day-Tripper and so terminates them before they can develop or grow into a being able to cause the bad spirit harm. Kill the children before they grow into soldiers, so to speak.

'Most Day-Trippers are like you were up until today. They see things flash by in the corner of their eyes and think they are just imagining it. They sense a presence, hear or smell something that is not expected to be in their current environment. They only get to know the truth if a Keeper has the need to come to them and explain. We Keepers will leave a potential Day-Tripper alone until we need them, so as not to alert any bad spirit of their true potential. However, we will always know who has the ability to one day be a Day-Tripper, and we will always keep an eye out for their safety. I'm very proud to say no Day-Tripper has been harmed on my watch.' Leonard couldn't help the smirk on his face as he spoke.

'What about my mum and dad?' grunted George.

Leonard's face dropped and he looked genuinely hurt by George's remark.

Granny quickly butted in, 'George, let Leonard finish, please.'

Leonard looked at her with a knowing smile, and continued.

'Thank you, dear lady. As your world is so large compared to the size of its population, and there are so few Day-Trippers on any world, it is obviously very rare for any to meet and even more rare for them to fall in love and marry. However, it appears your father also has the gene, and that makes you rather special.'

'ME! Special?' yawped George. 'How?'

'Because both of your parents are Day-Trippers,' beamed Leonard. 'I have never known this before.'

'So what does it mean?' asked George. 'Will I be a Keeper? Can I be a teacher? I always wanted to get my own back on our school teachers. "Sit down at the back, Chadbourn!"' shouted George, while doing an impression of Mr Chadbourn, his maths teacher. *Oh, how I'd love to get my own back on him*, he thought.

'I'm not sure about that,' quipped Leonard, 'but maybe one day! Only time will tell, and you have a long way to go before you are ready to take on the responsibility of being a Day-Tripper. For now, I need to help you to get used to what you can do with your new-found powers and teach you how to travel safely between worlds. Then we can start the search for your mum and dad.'

'POWERS!' shouted George. 'I have super-powers! That's great! Can I fly? Can I leap over tall buildings and catch bullets? Yay, let's get started!'

'Stop!' said both Granny and Leonard together.

'No, you can't fly, or leap over buildings, and you certainly can't catch a bullet – unless you want to die,' cautioned Leonard. 'And if you don't want to materialise into a solid wall and end up as part of a building, or fall through space for a few million years, I suggest we take our time and learn a few basic lessons first.'

Like most fourteen-year-olds, George was not good at waiting and even worse at learning lessons when he felt he had more exciting things to do. However, the thought of disappearing from this world and materialising in the middle of a wall was enough to slow him down long enough to listen to what Leonard had to say.

Over a plate of stew and dumplings, George and

Leonard went through the basics of inter-world travel. Well, Leonard *tried*! George was half-listening and half-daydreaming about flying through the air like Superman or swinging from building to building as if he were Spiderman.

'Remember how I explained travel between worlds was a bit like having thousands of planets connected by unseen tunnels?' said Leonard. 'Well, our first job is always to locate a tunnel doorway. Then, when we have a doorway, we need to know how to open it. After we have done those two things, we need to be able to find our chosen exit and look through to the other end to ensure we don't jump out and scare someone, or pop out into the path of an oncoming vehicle. Some doorways are in the middle of nowhere and some are in rather awkward and busy places.

'When the doorways were formed, many centuries ago, there were no roads or buildings on your planet. Some doorways have remained in quiet locations, but some are now in the middle of major cities. Some are inside buildings, or come out in the middle of a six-lane highway, so care is needed before anyone can just emerge into a different place.

'There are many thousands of tunnels, all integrated and connected in some way. A Keeper can plan their journey to go from one place and time, to wherever they need to be, however, because of the thousands of permutations and variables, it is very easy to take a wrong turn and get a little lost. When this happens, the Keeper must stop and check exactly where they are. They also need to check the coast is clear before they appear. It wouldn't do to just turn up out of nowhere in the middle of a crowded place, or frighten the life out of someone by just popping up beside them unannounced.'

'Is this what some people have seen when they think they've seen a ghost?' asked George.

'Well, yes, it could be,' acknowledged Leonard. 'I suppose that would be one explanation a human could give it. Well done! Good thinking, my boy.

'We all carry our master key,' he continued. 'In each time and place it looks different, so as to blend in. Here I have it as my pocket watch. Sometimes it's a wristwatch, sometimes a pen or a simple door key, and so on. The key allows us to keep track of people, spirits and what is going on in any world.'

'A bit like my iPad, or a tracker on a mobile phone, all integrated with Google maps?' interrupted George.

'I suppose so,' said Leonard. 'That is a good analogy, but quadrillions of times more powerful. It does have a small screen, so I can see what is outside the tunnel, but it has a very short range, hence I sometimes have to pop my head out, just to make sure all is clear. However, it's not my actual head that pops out, but a sort of hologram. If my real head popped out, I could lose it!'

'A Keeper can pop up anywhere for up to ten of your earthly seconds as a hologram, or to put it another way, they can appear as smoke or mist just for ten seconds. This is used to help them test where they are going if their usual view is blocked. It is usually when they are popping up in this format that future Day-Trippers think they have seen them. It also explains why some people are convinced they have seen a ghost or seen a ghostly figure move through a wall. It's easier for the lost Keeper to leave the poor victim thinking they have seen a ghost than to try to explain to an unsuspecting mortal exactly what I have just explained to you.

'Most people couldn't understand what is actually going on, and usually the Keeper doesn't have the time to hang about explaining. We are very busy people and always have so much to do,' protested Leonard, helping himself to his third bowl of stew and dumplings!

'It is also very important to note that, although a Keeper's natural life expectancy is far longer than a human, Keepers and Day-Trippers are not supermen. They can be killed on any world just like they can here on earth. Basically, we are all flesh and blood, just like you, so whilst it is their job to keep law and order, they must at all times be aware of their own mortality. Yes, Keepers can live for many centuries, but only if they keep safe.

'Human Day-Trippers still age, just like your granny has done. That is why they pass the gene down through generations, so their children can carry on the good work. However, when on a mission to other worlds, they do not age, regardless of the duration of the mission. When they come back, they are the same mortal age as when they left. When your grandmother was a teenager, she spent almost a year "off-world" with me, and was still exactly the same age when she returned a year later.'

'Let me get this straight,' said George. 'On other worlds you will age the same as the locals, but when you return to your world you will be the same age as when you left?'

'Exactly so,' grinned Leonard. 'It is like going back in time! The Creator didn't think it fair to use up some of your precious human lifespan doing his work on other worlds, so he made it possible for Day-Trippers to return to their original age when his work was done. However, on most occasions Day-Trippers are only away from their world for a few weeks at most, so no one notices they haven't aged along with the rest of humanity. Can you think of some people who don't look their age?'

'What, like Sir Cliff Richard?' chuckled George.

'Well, obviously I can't name names,' said Leonard, 'but most Day-Trippers have to be talented people to do the job. They also need to have human jobs that can allow them time off without people noticing, so they can do their day-tripping work without it impacting on their human lives and jobs.

'This is another reason why Day-Trippers are only used when absolutely necessary. It wouldn't do to keep giving mortal people extra years to live beyond what the Creator had originally granted them – that was not the Creator's idea when he made all the worlds.

'When speaking of the Creator I said "he", as people from your world think of the Creator as a male god who has made the human race in his own image. As no one has ever met the Creator, who are we to argue with your belief? However, as the rest of us are all spirits in our true form, if you are made in the Creator's image, then eventually you will return to a pure spirit form, a little like mist or smoke and bright light. Human form is of no use once you have returned to the Creator.'

George was getting confused and his head was spinning with all the sudden rush of information, so decided he needed to stick to the task of finding his parents. He could unravel the mysteries of what Leonard was trying to tell him when his mum and dad were safely back home, he mused.

'When I eventually find my parents, will they be exactly the same age as when they disappeared?' asked George.

'No. Well, yes, but no,' said Leonard. 'If you find them here on your world, they will be the same as the day they left, but if you find them on any other world they will have aged. They will only return to their original age when they return to this world. It all depends on where they have been for the last year.'

George's head was spinning. 'So, do you know where my mum and dad are. Can we go and get them?'

'Sort of,' cautioned Leonard. 'Sort of.'

'Sort of! What *sort of* answer is that?' shouted George, starting to lose his temper. 'Can you find them, or can't you?'

'George!' snapped Granny. 'Don't talk to Leonard like that. He is doing his best to explain.'

'Leonard, where – and when – are my daughter and son-in-law?'

'But—but, isn't that the same as I asked, and what do you mean "when"?' cried George.

Feeling like he was being attacked from both sides now, Leonard shook his head. He knew he needed to get on with the task at hand.

'Right, let me get to the real dangerous part of the lesson,' said Leonard firmly. 'Many centuries ago, a spirit was very bad, and upon his earthly death he had to be returned to the classroom for drastic work. He spent many years being taught right from wrong and the error of his ways. Eventually, his teachers decided he had learnt his lesson and was ready to be returned to human form, to be "born again" in your terms, so he could learn more earthly lessons and continue on his way to total enlightenment.

'The problem was, his condition was far worse than they thought. While he was up in the classroom supposedly learning his lesson, he was really only pretending to listen to his teachings. Unbeknown to his teacher, he was actually plotting how he could get back down to earth and once there prevent himself from ever returning to the classroom.

'Because our teachers consider all people to be

generally good at heart, with some just needing a little tweaking here and there, they tend to give all bad people the benefit of the doubt and believe they will all learn the true way eventually. So, when this particular bad spirit had been through the usual lessons, he was considered ready to return to your earth to continue with his quest to learn all the earth-bound life lessons and eventually be a fully enlightened spirit. He was therefore returned to earth to start a new human life.

'Once he had settled back on earth and completed his childhood, it soon became obvious through his terrible actions that he was still a bad spirit deep down. However, the Creator's failsafe was in place, and when his earthly life came to its end he was supposed to die and return to the classroom where drastic measures would be taken.

'The Creator gives life, he doesn't take it. However, on vary rare occasions it is deemed necessary to return a bad spirit to the classroom early to prevent further damage to the world it inhabits.

'A plan was put in place to return the spirit to the classroom, but they had underestimated the cunning and power of the evil spirit. He had no intention of being killed and returned for more corrective training.

'No spirit had ever attempted to stop itself from returning before. How could they? Spirits have no idea of the spirit world and where they are going after death. Yes, many have tried to avoid death, that's a normal human trait. However, until now no one had the ability to do anything about it. After all, that would require a spirit avoiding death, and no one can avoid death – it's inevitable in the end.

'The spirit's mental capacity was far greater than any before. He not only found a way to retain his memory from his previous human life, but also from his spirit life and attempted retraining. He knew we would come after him and had devised a plan to find a weak-willed individual who would not have the mental capacity to protect his mind from the evil spirits thoughts. All he needed was to keep his weak-willed human servant very close at all times, as timing would be critical.

'His plan was to try to avoid death until it became impossible for him to continue in his current body, because all human bodies fail eventually. At that point, seconds before his earthly life became extinct, he managed to use his newly acquired mental skills to make his spirit leave his body and change places with the spirit of the weak-willed human standing next to him. When the bad spirit's old body died, the other spirit returned to the classroom and the bad spirit continued to live in the second spirit's body.'

'WHAT?!' exclaimed George. 'He can become anyone he wants and they die instead of him?'

'Err, yes – but they have to be willing.'

Leonard was now trying to justify how this had been allowed to happen.

'Throughout your history, all tyrants have had slaves willing to give their lives for their masters. This has never been done before and it caught everyone out. No spirit had ever even attempted to stop itself from returning – it's unprecedented. As I said, spirits have no idea of the spirit world or where they are going after their "human death".

'As soon as the wrong spirit appeared in the classroom, we knew something was terribly wrong. The wrong spirit had been prematurely returned to the classroom and the bad spirit was still down on earth inhabiting his new human body.

'Having achieved this once, we assumed he could do it again and again, each time growing mentally stronger. The bad spirit could now be almost immortal, changing bodies each time something happens to his current body. This was never a part of the Creator's plan.

'Over the last few centuries, he pops up throughout history in many guises and with many names. From time to time someone, often a Keeper, manages to defeat him, but when this happens he simply transfers into an alternative body. All he has to do is always surround himself – or herself, as the spirit has inhabited many human bodies, both male and female, over time – with weak-minded individuals who he/she can exchange bodies with when the body he/she is inhabiting finally succumbs to human extinction.

'He/she knows if his spirit is forced back to the classroom for a teacher to teach him the good ways, he could be changed for ever, because the next time the teacher will not let him back to earth until he has learned his lesson properly, and if the teacher is not happy that the job has been done they will never release him. For him to ensure he stays "bad", he has to avoid going back to the classroom.

'This was supposed to be the Creator's failsafe. When any spirit turned bad, no matter how bad they became, they would always eventually die. And when they die, they go back to the Creator's classroom to be taught and "reprogrammed", to use a modern phrase, to get them back on the path to being good and true.

'The Creator was never really worried about a spirit using their given right or "free will" to choose the wrong path for ever throughout eternity, as he always has the ability to change and re-educate them at the end of each earthly life, and your earthly life has a rather short lifespan compared to eternity.

'The Creator thought he had the ultimate failsafe, and for many centuries, he had!

'We are still not sure how this evil spirit manages to move from body to body when he dies, or how he chooses his new host. We know he must always have hand-picked disciples standing by ready to change places with him, should something happen that threatens his earth body.

'We don't know if these disciples are aware of the sacrifice they are making, or if he tricks them into surrendering their body as and when he needs it, although for centuries your kings and rulers have had faithful disciples who are ready to give their lives for their lord and master. Your history shows that many slaves' bodies have been found buried in pyramids alongside their kings.

'If we are to ever stop this evil spirit and have any chance to re-educate him, we need to surround him with people who are not willing to sacrifice their mortal lives so he can live on. Then we can catch him and return him to the classroom as soon as possible, before he can jump into another body.

'We have given him the name of Roman, as his first reincarnation coincided with your Roman Empire period, and it was as a fierce gladiator that he first came to our notice.

'One suggestion as to how he keeps jumping from one mortal body to another is that he can somehow sense a fellow Day-Tripper, but one that has never been initiated into our group. He uses their special life force to keep him alive. It's as if he feeds off their special spirit strength and this gives him more power each time he transfers into another human body. As they are unaware of their powers as a Day-Tripper, they do not realise their importance to him.

'This is where you come in George. Sadly, because you are the child of two parents who both hold the special Keeper gene, you are extra-special and we feel you are a strong target for a future body exchange as and when Roman requires it.'

'WHAT!!!' screamed George. 'He can't have my body, I haven't finished with it yet!'

'It's all right, George,' Leonard comforted him. 'I am here to protect you. Now let's get on with the lesson and then we can start looking for your parents. With them back home safe and sound, you will have me, your grandmother and both parents looking out for you. Even Roman can't get through all four of us.'

George looked at his grandmother. He could tell by the look of love in her eyes that he was safe, at least for now.

'Right,' said Leonard in a commanding voice, 'as a Keeper we can look like anything on any planet, but we aren't really that person or object,' and suddenly morphed into an exact copy of George!

George gasped at seeing himself standing before him. Leonard then transformed into the TV and then into Milly the dog before returning to his original form.

Shaking his head, Leonard said, 'You see, I looked like you, but if I had died while looking like you, it would have been me who died, not you. You and your spirit were in front of me and you would have remained standing there regardless of what happened to me.

'The evil spirit has managed to go beyond just looking like someone else. He doesn't just look like another person, he somehow manages to push the person's spirit out of their body, and replaces it with his own spirit, so he actually *becomes* that person, while their spirit goes into his old body, usually just seconds before the body dies! Do you see why we have to stop him?

'There are exceptions to the rule. From time to time, when some spirits die, they don't return to the classroom straight away. For example, if the spirit has been exceptionally good, has a strong mental aura and was not ready to die at their allotted time because they felt they had more good work to do, they may try to stay on earth to finish what they started. Or, if they died in a dramatic or particularly alarming way, they may need to come to terms with their bodily death before they are accepting of their fate. On these occasions, they may remain on earth in a spirit form for a short period to allow the spirit time to adjust. This is allowed because it has been proven to help with their teaching when they do finally return. Their minds are ready and more accepting of their new teachings.

'Last year, an experienced Day Tripper died, but the spirit had not arrived back in the classroom. Your parents were sent on a mission to find the spirit, and help it find peace and show it the way home. We think they were unwittingly sent to a body that had been replaced by Roman the spirit, who is moving from body to body. The bad spirit must have been aware they were looking for him and could not afford to be caught red-handed by two such intrepid Keepers. His life was on the line and he certainly wasn't in any mood to give up.'

'So where are my parents?' George cried. 'Are they dead?'

'Well, I don't think so, as their spirits never arrived back in the classroom either,' confessed Leonard.

'Has the bad spirit taken them over? Are my parents bad now?' said George in a croaking voice. He couldn't help his tears.

'Again, we don't think so. They have an aura that we can usually trace. All spirits have their own aura: it is like their life-source and we can usually trace it like a beacon. That is how we usually find people. Remember, a free spirit can move around at his or her own discretion. We can still feel your parents' aura, but it isn't strong enough to get a trace on, hence I cannot find them without your help.'

'Okay, let's do it! When, where and how do we start?' said George eagerly.

'Fabulous! beamed Leonard. 'This is the plan, George: place your hand on the wall and see if it feels solid to you.'

'Of course it's solid,' said George. 'It's a wall!'

'Yes, I know it's a wall,' Leonard responded, 'but I'm going to open the door into the multiverse corridors, so you can experience what it is like to move a few feet within a time-and multiverse travel tunnel. Now, place your hand slowly against the wall.'

'Careful,' cautioned Granny. 'We don't want to lose you as well.'

George turned towards his granny and smiled.

'Don't worry, Gran, I can't fall into a wall and get lost. And anyway, Leonard said he has never lost anyone on his watch.'

At that exact moment, Milly came bounding through the door and pushed it straight into George's face. Grabbing his face with both hands, he reeled around and fell backwards, straight through the unseen opening in the wall.

'George!' shouted Leonard and Granny at the same time.

'Oh, ecky thump,' exclaimed Leonard. 'That's never

happened before. He doesn't know where he is going! And we don't know where he has gone either. Oh my, oh my, oh my. Where will the darling boy end up?'

'Well, get him back!' shouted Granny. 'And quick. He has no idea where he is going or what to expect.'

'Neither have I,' admitted Leonard. 'I was just opening the portal to show him how it works, then Milly burst in! I didn't dial in any destination!'

'So where HAS he gone?' squealed Granny.

'Erm, I've no idea,' said Leonard.

'I think I should go after him,' said Granny, rolling up her sleeves.

'No! This is all my fault. You stay here, I will check my files to see if I can narrow down the options of where he may be and then I'll go after him.'

With that, Leonard nervously twiddled with his pocket-watch master key.

Granny did what all grown-ups do at a time of emergency: she shot into the kitchen and put the kettle on for a cup of strong tea.

Leonard's fingers were quickly scrolling through the screen on his pocket-watch database. 'It's no good, Elizabeth, I think I'm just going to have to dive in and search for him the good old-fashioned way. Wait here, I'll be back as quickly as I can, and let's hope I can find him before that evil creature Roman does.'

George's grandmother spun around. 'Oh, please hurry and find him, Leonard. You must bring him back.'

With a smile and a wink, Leonard jumped through the portal doorway and disappeared.

Meanwhile, George was tumbling along as if he were flying, but in slow motion, about as fast as a gentle jog. He was travelling through what felt like a white tunnel with smooth walls. Every ten to fifteen feet he could see an oval opening. Each opening was like an open door or window with no glass and appeared to lead through something like a doorway to another place. He could recognise some of the sights, but others looked very different to what he was used to seeing on earth. Because there were no doors on the openings, George felt he could just jump through any one at any time, but first he would have to slow down a little more.

Come on, George, he said to himself. *What's the best thing to do? Just float around in this tunnel for who knows how long, or take a chance and jump through one of the openings and hope I can pop up back in Granny's kitchen.*

George thought long and hard. *What's the chances with so many openings that I will end up back where I want to be?* he mused. *If I stay here, Leonard can* come and get me. Surely, he is somewhere behind me. Surely, he is coming after me.

George tried to turn around and look behind him, but although he was moving slowly, he hadn't yet got the hang of manoeuvring himself around.

He made a grab for one of the openings, hoping he could use it to stop his flight and maybe use it to anchor himself, so he could turn around to see if Leonard was behind him, but couldn't get a grip. He put his feet out to try to push off one side of the wall, so he could get his finger tips closer to the next opening, but his feet slipped on the smooth walls. *C'mon George,* he said to himself. *Stop messing about and grab the damn thing.*

His rebuke to himself worked. He managed to get sufficient grip to slow himself down long enough to grab at the doorway. He slammed his feet against the wall and tightened his fingers around the top of the opening.

To his amazement, his fingers seemed to disappear from sight. He slowly pushed more of his hand into the opening. It too disappeared. He let go and pulled his hand back out again, his fingers were still there!

Right, he thought, *maybe I could grab the next opening and pop my head through to have a look to see where I am?*

He pushed off the wall with his feet again and felt like a spaceman floating about weightless in space. The next opening was just in front of him, so he reached out and grabbed at the sides, his fingers locked onto the side. Once he had a firm hold, he slowly poked his head through the opening.

Before his eyes could focus, poor old George's eardrums were almost split by the shriek and screaming coming from just in front of him.

'It's a head, a dead boy's head floating in space,' a voice cried out, and then began screaming even louder than before.

George quickly pulled his head back inside the tunnel and let go. He was floating along again, his heart pumping like it was trying to jump out of his body.

Crickey, he said to himself, *Leonard told me about popping up in another place without looking first, but how do I look, I don't have one of those pocket-watch thingamabobs like Leonard does. Oh Leonard, Granny, where are you? How am I ever going to find my way home?*

George rolled into a ball and continued to float along the tunnel thinking about his day and all the new information he had been given. After a few moments he opened his eyes.

Pull yourself together, he muttered to himself. *This is the adventure of a lifetime, make the most of it.* He may not have asked for the day he had been given, but he thought he may as well make the most of it.

Wow, he thought, *I never expected this when I got out*

of bed this morning! Just wait until I tell Charlie where I've been, he'll never believe it! It's better than playing cricket.

George managed to turn around by pushing off the sides of the walls with his hands and feet. His heart rate was returning to normal and he felt a little calmer now. He could at least control his movements, but there was no sign of Leonard, and rescue.

I think my best bet would be to try to stop and wedge myself in, so that Leonard can come along and get me. If I pop into another world, he may never find me. I may never see my parents again, my granny, Milly, all gone for ever, he agonised.

Then his thoughts came back into the moment. He could hear a swooshing noise as if someone was sliding towards him through the tunnel. *Oh my, who is it? What is it? Please let it be Leonard and not Roman, or I'm dead.*

George looked around him. He was right next to one of the door openings. *I don't think I can take the risk of just waiting here to be caught, I have to get back and help find Mum and Dad.*

George reached out and grabbed the edge of the next opening and with a push from his feet slipped out of the tunnel and through to the other side. He landed unceremoniously on his backside with a *plop!*

The first thing he noticed was the cold. The temperature in the tunnel had been nice and warm, now he was feeling very cold. It wasn't totally dark, but it was very gloomy. His mind started racing. *Where am I? And where is Leonard?*

George peered through the gloom to see if he was alone. He couldn't see anything, or anyone, but at least no one was screaming at him this time.

He looked around to see where the door opening had

gone – fully aware that he may need to get out again quickly. The floor was damp, but just where he had been sitting, he found a warm patch. Perhaps, until Leonard taught him another way, this was one way for him to find one of the doorways: they may be warmer than on the world he was visiting.

A little frightened and a little excited, George stood up and started to move forward to see if he could work out where he was. *Am I on my earth?* he thought. *Or another planet completely? When is it? Am I in the future or the past?*

Part of him wanted to be whisked back to his granny's kitchen and the warmth of her cuddles, and cakes. But another part of him was a little excited at the prospect of adventure – an adventure most boys could never even dream of.

Crack! George jumped at the sound, his heart pounding as his blood surged through his body, preparing him for fight, flight or freeze. He wanted to cry out 'Who's there?' but the words wouldn't come out. Then he heard it again. It was the sound of someone – or something – walking towards him and stepping carefully, but not carefully enough, on the twigs lying on the ground.

A foul smell seared up through George's nostrils. It was enough to make him sick, but he knew his best bet was to try to stay quiet and still, so as not give away his position. Who knows, it may be possible that whoever – whatever – it is hasn't noticed him. They surely wouldn't be able to smell him over the smell they are giving off, he thought.

Then, as his eyes started to get used to the dimmed light, he could make out the eerie sight before him.

Standing approximately twenty feet in front of him

where five huge animals. They resembled wolves, but each of them was at least as big as a large horse. Their size and bulk reminded George of the shire horses he used to see in his home village on special parade days, but far more frightening. Their jaws were wide open showing off a terrifying array of enormous teeth with drool dripping from every one. The smell of their breath was now so bad it was almost impossible for George to stop himself from choking.

One of the animals, the biggest one, had what looked like blood dripping from its shoulder, and George could see it was in pain.

His mind was spinning, what should he do, he thought.

Run – but where to?

Stay and see what happens, and possibly be torn limb from limb and then eaten?

He felt in his pockets to see if he could find something to give him any ideas. All he had was a handkerchief and his pocketknife. *Not exactly an armoury*, he thought. George started moving backwards very slowly, hoping he could just drop through the doorway and into the tunnel before the wolves could reach him, but he just backed into a large tree with a bump.

'Grrrrr,' the wolves gave off a growl loud enough to frighten an army of soldiers, let alone a fourteen-year-old boy all alone.

The biggest beast moved slowly towards him. George froze on the spot. As it got closer, he could clearly see the blood on its shoulder. A large pointed piece of wood like an arrow was sticking out of the wound and the animal was obviously in distress.

I'm going to be eaten alive, thought George, shaking so hard his teeth were starting to rattle. *Wait! Perhaps if it will let me take the arrow out of his shoulder it'll leave me alone, like the lion in the story where it has a thorn removed from its paw*, he thought. *But how do I get close enough to remove it without being eaten?*

The lion in the story sat back and let the thorn be removed from its paw. These creatures didn't look like the sort who would just sit back, at least not until they had satisfied their hunger, and George was on the menu!

Come on George, think, he said to himself. *Okay, I have two options, stand still and get eaten, or have a go at removing the arrow and at least have a chance of saving myself*, he thought. *Oh man, how did I get myself into this? A few minutes ago, I was standing in Granny's kitchen and now I'm on a different planet about to be eaten by an enormous wolf!* Sweat was running down his back.

With a jump that would have impressed an Olympic athlete, he leapt up at the wolf's shoulder. The wolf, taken aback by such swift and unexpected movement, and totally unaware of George's good intentions tried to bite at him, but his neck was so big he couldn't get his jaws around to his own shoulder. George felt like his nose would melt from the strength of the foul smell from the wolf's breath, but he knew what he had to do.

George grabbed a fistful of hair and clung on for all he was worth. Once he had a firm hold, he let go with one hand, seized the arrow and pulled with all his might. It wouldn't budge, but it was obviously hurting the wolf and it screamed in pain.

The other wolves stepped back at the sound and sight of what they must have thought was their leader being attacked. Then they gathered their composure and moved in for the kill!

George let go of the fur and put both hands on the

arrow. He braced himself against the wolf's neck with both feet and pulled with both hands as if his very life depended on it.

With a sickening squelch the arrow came free and George fell backwards to the ground still holding the arrow.

The wolf squealed in pain, but knew he was finally free of the arrow that could have caused his death if it hadn't been removed. He sat back and stared at George, as if deciding what to do with him.

Looking up at the wolf George felt a slight pang of relief, until he saw the other four wolves coming straight at him!

He may have helped save the life of the lead wolf, but the other four were still hungry and were not in the least bit grateful for what George had done. All they could see was a tasty meal sitting on the floor in front of them, and they were ready to eat.

As they came straight at him, George's heart was pounding harder than ever before. The saliva from the wolves' foul mouths was now so close he could feel it warm and wet against his face.

George grabbed two handfuls of soil. *This is it*, he thought. *I'm going to die here and I don't even know where here is. I'm going to be eaten and no one will ever find me because there won't be anything to find.*

The first wolf was just inches from George's face, it opened its mouth wide enough to take in as much of George as it could. He knew what he didn't get in his mouth with the first bite, the other three would get, so he only had one chance to eat his fill.

George tried to throw the handful of soil into the animal's eyes, but he was so frightened that he couldn't lift either arm. He just lay on the grass, their slimy drool dripping onto his trousers. George closed his eyes; he couldn't bear to look. He felt the nose touch his forehead. The wolf's teeth were closing around his head.

Then, in an instant, he felt something grab at his shirt collar from behind. A ghostly hand had reached out from the doorway and pulled him back through, just in the nick of time.

'Leonard!' George shouted. 'Thank you, oh thank you, you saved me from being eaten!'

He grabbed Leonard around the waist and hugged him with all his might. But quick he cried, the wolves will come and get us. We've got to get away, now!'

'What on earth is the matter with you, George? I told you, only Keepers can move through the tunnels. The wolves can't get through – you're safe. It has taken me quite a while to locate you, young man. What on earth were you doing on that world? It has a reputation for being a dangerous place, you know. You should choose your vacation places with a little more care.'

George jumped to his knees. He couldn't help himself from crying, he was so happy to be back.

'Hold on to me,' said Leonard. 'Let's get you back to your grandmother.' And with a whoosh they both flew off back up the tunnels to the warmth and safety of Granny's kitchen.

CHAPTER 4

George Goes Off-World

Leonard, George and Granny were sitting around the table in the kitchen, their stomachs full of cake, scones with jam and cream, and lots of hot tea.

George looked at Leonard. He could see the reflection of his grandmother in Leonard's eyes, however it was her, but not as he knew her. To George, his granny was just like any other granny: soft grey hair, a wrinkled face with a few little fluffy hairs, especially on her chin. Slightly built, but with a soft chubby middle where George liked to put his head when they were having a cuddle on the sofa. Yet in the eyes of Leonard she was a beautiful dark-haired girl of no more than nineteen with a straight back and solid form.

He had never seen his granny like this. She had always been old ever since the day he was born, but now he could see her as Leonard saw her all those years ago. George had a feeling that he almost recognised the young woman he could see reflecting in Leonard's eyes. She reminded him of the girl at the cricket match – the one no one else had seen!

He turned to look at her and she smiled back at him. 'I was young once, George, but that was a long time ago. I would love to come with you, but I'm afraid I cannot. Age, and the aching bones it brings, has caught up with me and I would only hold you back. Go with Leonard and bring my daughter back to me. Always do as he tells you. Never disobey him, as he is there to look after you and make sure you all hurry back. It's crumpets for tea!

Shall I make your favourite jelly and ice cream for afters?'

George smiled. He would normally love the thought of his favourite strawberry jelly and ice cream for tea, but right now his mind was set on one thing. Finding Mum and Dad!

Leonard walked over to the invisible door and held out his hand to George, who took it firmly. They both slipped through the door and in a blink of an eye they were both flying through space.

George's head felt like it was going to explode. 'Don't hold your breath!' shouted Leonard. 'Breathe normally and it will be fine.'

It doesn't feel fine, thought George. *How long are we going to be?* He didn't have to wait long!

Bump! they landed on a hard surface. George's face felt like it had been slapped hard by a huge hand and his bottom didn't feel much better.

'Where are we?' moaned George, rubbing his face.

'It's all right, little man. I just needed to pop ahead to make sure we were safe to land.'

'But how could you have done?' said George. 'I was holding your hand all the time.'

'Ah, you *thought* you were,' chortled Leonard, with a smug grin on his face. 'You will have to start getting used to the unusual, as the normal rules do not apply from now on.'

George looked across at where Leonard's voice was coming from. It was Leonard, but he was now just over six feet tall, had dark hair and looked more like James Bond than the Jiminy Cricket figure George had become used to seeing.

'What happened to you?' exclaimed George, his head moving up and down as he examined the new Leonard.

'I have to take the form of the locals, George, or

someone will soon notice I am not from this world.'

George stopped staring at Leonard and looked about him. They appeared to be in a big room, a little like a church, but without any of the usual church items. Just a big empty room with a high ceiling, stone floor and a few wooden benches.

'This is one of my favourite places to think,' said Leonard. 'It's what you may call a "safe house", a special place where Keepers can come to be alone with their thoughts. Because the floor is so hard most Keepers will not come here, as they prefer a soft landing.'

'So this is the place you decided to bring me on my first flight,' grumbled George. 'Thanks for nothing. My bottom and legs are stiff from landing so hard and my face feels like it's been slapped.'

At that moment there was a bang on the large oak doors. George almost jumped out of his skin.

'Who is it? You said this was a safe house.'

'I'm good,' retorted Leonard sarcastically, 'but I don't possess X-ray vision. Let's open the door and we will find out.'

He opened the door a few inches so he could peer around it to see who it was.

Bang! It flew open and four large men dressed all in black burst in. Three of them grabbed Leonard, while the fourth got hold of George and spun him around. Even with Leonard's new bulky form, he was no match for all four of them.

Leonard stared at the men. They were all over six feet tall, heavily built and wearing black boots, black jeans and black bomber jackets with black woolly hats. One was at the front and obviously the leader.

'What do you want?' demanded Leonard.

'Be quiet!' the lead man said. 'If you want to live.'

'Sit the Keeper down,' he instructed the other men, 'and keep an eye on him, he can move very quickly.'

The lead man sneered at Leonard: 'Who is the boy?'

'Let the boy go!' barked Leonard. 'He was just in here sheltering from the rain. He is of no use to you and you don't want to alert the local police by taking a hostage, do you?'

George felt like screaming, but something inside him knew to keep quiet. If they let him go, it would be up to him to help Leonard. He had only been off-world for a few minutes and already he was in trouble and it looked like it could be up to him to save the day.

The lead man nodded to the man holding George. 'Get rid of the kid,' he said.

The man holding George put his hand over George's mouth. 'Don't make a sound, boy,' he said. 'Don't come back and don't mention anything to anyone, or I will come looking for you. Okay?'

George nodded as if to agree to the man's terms, although he didn't have much of an alternative.

The man opened the big door, grabbed George by the scruff of his neck and threw him out. George landed heavily on the hard cobbles. He turned to hear the man say, 'Go, boy, and speak to no one, or you'll regret it!'

Then he turned and slammed the big door shut behind him.

There was a low stone wall all around the building and George was small enough to hide behind it. He started to run as he had been told, but, as soon as he was out of sight behind the wall, he stopped and looked back.

What was he going to do now? He couldn't fetch help – for a start, he had no idea where he was. Was he even still on planet earth? His bedroom was full of superhero comics. *What would they do?* thought George, then shook his head hard. It was no time for daydreaming, Leonard was in trouble!

The landscape was unfamiliar to George, but it still looked like earth. Earth, but a long way from Derbyshire! Could he look for a policeman? Would the locals understand him? Oh, where was his granny when he needed her.

There was a lot of shouting coming from inside the building. He crept a little closer to see if he could find out what was going on. Lifting his head just high enough to peer over the wall, he fixed his eyes on one of the large windows. He was just getting used to the light when he felt a hand across his mouth and an arm around his neck pulling him to the ground.

George's heart sank. He had been captured again and they certainly wouldn't let him go so easily this time. What would Leonard think of him? He had let everyone down.

'Shush,' said a soft voice. 'We don't want them to hear us, do we?'

George looked up into the eyes of a beautiful girl. She was about sixteen or seventeen, but strong, and with a note of experience in her voice that made her sound much older than her years.

'Who are you?' asked George. 'Shush, I said, or you will get us both caught.'

The girl signalled for George to follow her.

Slowly and quietly, they both crawled back towards the big door. George's heart was still banging so hard he was sure everyone could hear it.

The girl hid behind the door and made a tapping motion to George.

'You want me to knock the door? They will hear me,' he whispered.

'That's the plan. Now, do it.'

'Plan? What plan? I didn't know we had a plan,' whispered George.

'Just do it,' she ordered, with a grimace on her face.

George knew she meant business, so he tapped the door as she had asked him, all the time thinking he was mad to do so. After all, he had just escaped, why would he want to go back in there, even with this young girl with him? How could that help?

The door flung open and the man looked down at a petrified George.

'You!' he exclaimed. 'What do you want? I knew you were trouble.'

At that point the girl spun around the door brandishing a wooden pole. She knocked the first man down and almost flew into the room as if she were pole-vaulting. She crashed into the second man, who was running towards the open door. She attacked him like some Ninja warrior princess and he was soon lying flat out on the hard floor.

George looked across at where Leonard was sitting. While his two guards were staring wide-eyed at what was coming through the door, Leonard jumped up and grabbed the arm of the man beside him. He flung him around into the face of the other man. There was a loud smack as they came face to face at speed, and with a sickly splat they were both lying on the floor, unconscious.

George just stood in amazement at what he had just witnessed. Leonard was dragging all four men into a heap on the floor while the girl tied them up.

'Welcome to the quest, George,' he panted. 'I see you have already met Beth. Don't worry, she is a very old friend.'

CHAPTER 5

George Starts to Understand

The three of them sat on the benches in the big hall. George hadn't noticed at first, but the once-empty room now had furniture and a large open roaring fire on the back wall.

'How did that happen?' enquired George, with an astonished look on his face. 'And where did Beth come from? How did she know we were here?'

'It's all right, Georgie,' said Beth. 'It will all come clear soon.'

'Georgie?' he repeated. 'Only my mum and granny call me that. Who are you? How do you know me? And where are we?'

'Well, don't you worry about that now. You have far more things to concern yourself with, like helping us to find your mum and dad.'

'Are you hungry?' asked Leonard.

Food was usually uppermost in George's mind, however today he had been so caught up in his real-life 'cops and robbers' game, that he hadn't given it a second thought. But now someone had mentioned it, he *was* hungry!

'Yes,' he replied, 'but where can we find food out here?'

Beth walked out of the large room and into a side room. Within what felt like seconds, she returned with three plates of food. It was warm and smelt delicious. It looked like slices of pizza with warm cheese dripping off the sides, hot cross buns with butter and strawberry jam and a pot of hot tea. Maybe not the most health-conscious food, but to a very hungry George it was a banquet.

'Where did you get that?' George asked. 'Is there a café through there?'

'You don't need to concern yourself about where it came from, Georgie. Just eat up and enjoy it.'

George felt he knew the mysterious Beth. She was familiar, but he had no idea where he had met her before.

'Do you go to my school?' George asked politely.

Beth smiled. 'Well, I did once.'

'Ah, so that's where I know you from is it. Are you a Keeper or a Day-Tripper?'

'I am impressed you know so much about us already. You must have been paying attention when Leonard was explaining it all to you. Now eat up, as we need to get going before Roman sends some more of his men to find us.'

'Hang on, I've got it! You were the girl who helped me catch the ball at the cricket match.'

'Helped you catch a cricket ball?' Beth queried with a knowing smile. 'Wouldn't it be illegal if two people caught it? Anyway, I'm a girl, and I don't play cricket!'

George screwed his face up. He knew he had seen Beth before, and he was sure she was the girl at the cricket match that had stopped time so he could prevent the ball from hitting the baby. However, he didn't want to make a fuss and have her ridicule him. Even after all that had happened today, he was still uncertain how they would react to him discussing time standing still, so he decided to leave it – for now.

'What do we know about this Roman bloke?' asked George.

'We think he has been moving from body to body for centuries. The first time we actually worked out what he was doing was during the occupation of the Roman Empire. He was a gladiator who rose to power through his almost superhuman feats of bravery and prowess in the amphitheatres and on the battlefields. Hence we named him "Roman", after the first era during which he came to our attention.

'At the time, no one had any idea that he had worked out how, as he was dying, he could move his spirit from his own body into someone else's body. No doubt this knowledge was how he managed to show such bravery in battle. It has to help if you know you are immortal!

'I will not give names to all the earthly people he has embodied, so as not to confuse you with the history you know, or think you know, but suffice it to say, where a monster has risen amongst humankind to try to wreak havoc and ruin all mankind, Roman is sure to be found at the heart of the trouble.'

'What does he look like?' asked George.

'Ah,' said Beth. 'You were not listening to Leonard quite as well as I thought, were you? As a Keeper, he can transform into any being or object he wishes, but only for short periods. However, with his newly developed skill, he is not just transforming how he looks to the outside world. When humans die, their spirit leaves the body and goes back up to the classroom to meet their teacher. The body is left on earth to be cremated, or buried, so it can go back to nature through decomposition, like a plant would. The spirit leaves the body a few seconds before the body actually dies, and, in the case of people who are experiencing a traumatic or painful death, the spirit can leave a second or two earlier so as not to suffer unnecessarily. 'We think Roman died somehow and went back to the classroom, as all spirits do, for reflection and teaching before being reborn later as a new human life. When a new life is born, it is not supposed to be able to remember anything of their previous spirit life until after their next human death, when they are safely back in the spirit world. Once they return there, they can experience all their previous lives, so they can use their past experiences to help them become a fully enlightened spirit, which is of course the optimum goal.

'The next time Roman died was on a battlefield, along with many other soldiers. It would appear his spirit was able to leave his mortal body just before it perished, but instead of returning to the spirit world classroom, it somehow managed to jump into a nearby healthy body, pushing out the body's spirit and forcing it into his old dying body. The other person's spirit would then return prematurely, leaving Roman's spirit alive and well in the new body.

'We have looked back at all the data and it would appear that, when Roman was dying from his battle wounds, he was embraced by a deep and close friend who was holding him and crying at the death of his comrade.

'Whether Roman changed places with his friend intentionally, or it just happened with one dying in the arms of a close loved one who may at that exact time have been wishing it was he who had been killed instead, we will never know. However, what we do know is, it was the friend who returned while Roman remained on earth in his friend's body.

'This was the first time it had ever happened and Roman must have decided there and then that this was his opportunity for eternal life on earth, if he could manage to work out how it happened and ensure that someone who loved or cared for him was always nearby when mortal death approached him.

'Roman knew he had one more lifetime to work out how to do it, and if he could, he would never have to return to the spirit world. Somehow, he managed it and has now been doing it for centuries, although, with each transformation from one body to another, he loses some of his spirit power. We think he is getting very weak now and we were expecting him to soon lose enough power for us to prevent him from making the switch, thus forcing him back up to the classroom, where he will be restrained and dealt with. We now believe he has learned that, if he can jump into the body of a Keeper, the Keeper's extra power rejuvenates him, as he can feed on their much stronger spirit.

'You are special, George, as you are the offspring of not just one Keeper, but two. With the extra energy your spirit has, and Roman's life force fading at every transformation, we think you are going to be a target he cannot resist. Sorry to be the bearer of bad news, Georgie, but you could be his next victim.

'We have been keeping an eye on you and helping to keep you safe since your birth, but as you grow, so does your inner spirit, and it is this spirit that has been attracting Roman like a moth to a light. It is now so strong, we feel it is only a matter of time before he finds you. If this happens, not only will we lose you, but Roman will become so strong it could be centuries before we can trap him again – centuries during which he will be able to wreak havoc amongst all humankind.

'Roman could sense your spirit, but was having difficulty tracing you due to a spirit damper we had around you. Your parents and grandmother were responsible for maintaining your safety and they were doing a great job. Unable to find you directly, Roman came up with a cunning plan. He decided he could find you through your parents, but when he found them and they would not give up your whereabouts, he decided to keep them hidden, so you would come to him.'

'What?!' exclaimed George. 'What has he done to them? Has he hurt them? Has he tortured them just to find me?'

George was shaking with fear and rage. He couldn't help crying at the thought of what had become of his beloved parents.

'Don't cry, Georgie,' Beth tried to reassure him. 'We have been monitoring the situation as best we can, and although their spirit signal is too weak for us to get a direct fix on, we can sense their spirit aura is still alive and strong. That means they have not been harmed, and Roman knows he needs to keep them alive if he is to use them as bait to trap you.

'Roman is now getting a little too close for comfort and we need to return him to the classroom as soon as possible, so he can be confined to the spirit world before he can use your strength to potentially start World War III! With your aura added to his already formidable powers and knowledge, he would make the sort of opponent your world has never experienced before, and a mighty foe to any spirit tasked with catching him. We must do all we can to stop him before he can feed off your spirit.'

'Am I bait?' asked George with a croak in his voice. 'Have you brought me here so Roman can come and get me, is that it?'

'No, Georgie. That is far from the truth. We would never let him have you, and the world could not afford the devastation he could wreak if he got double power from your essence. If he ever achieved this transformation, he could be too strong for us - this is why we have taken a vow to protect you. We know he is close to finding out where you are and is closing in on you, hence we sent Leonard to bring you to safety. However, it looks like he knows about this place and it is time to move again.'

'Where is this place?' queried George.

'It's a different dimension from where you were born. It looks like earth and has all the same air, water, earth, rock, minerals, etc, but it is slightly different from the earth you grew up in.'

'How many dimensions are there?' George asked, with a look of bewilderment on his face.

'Hundreds of thousands,' interjected Leonard. 'You now know you are able to move from one to another by use of the portals - something only Keepers can do - but through the taking of potential Keepers' bodies over the years, Roman has gained some of their powers to move through time and space, just as we can. We are not completely sure what he can and cannot do, and where his powers end. We know he has moved to some alternate worlds, but we think he is limited and cannot go everywhere, or stay there for long. However, this is just what we think through our investigations so far. We are not sure. What we *are* sure of is, if he gets your extra powers, he will certainly be a much stronger force than he is now! Are you ready?'

'Ready? Ready for what?' asked George.

'Ready to catch Roman and find your parents.'

'You betcha,' said George forthrightly. 'Bring him on!'

CHAPTER 6

Time for Battle

'Beth,' said George. 'You said you sent Leonard to me, but he says he is thousands of years old and you are only a kid, so how...'

'Don't let it get to you, Georgie. Time is not how you think of it: I can appear fifteen or one hundred and fifty in the blink of an eye. Just keep your thoughts on your mum and dad. If you concentrate hard enough, you may be able to pick up on their aura and we can use that to find them. If we find them, we should find Roman. You'll get your mum and dad back and we will capture Roman once and for all.'

George looked bewildered, but not wishing to hold everything up, he got up and followed Beth and Leonard out of the building into the twilight.

'Shouldn't we stay here until morning?' George said with a squeak in his voice. 'I'm not afraid of the dark or anything, but is it safe to go out at night when people are after us?'

'I understand your concerns, George,' whispered Leonard. 'But we need to look for a safer shelter before Roman turns up. By now, he will know his men have failed and that will trigger him to send more to look for them – and us!'

At the end of the drive stood a small black car. It looked like a typical 4x4 SUV, but a bit smaller than the ones George was used to seeing on the farms in Derbyshire. Leonard climbed into the driver's seat and Beth opened the rear door for George to get in.

'Erm, I get carsick in the back,' George protested. 'Can I sit in the front with Leonard please?'

Beth looked at him. 'I'm afraid your earthly travel sicknesses cannot be allowed to put you in danger here, Georgie. Get in the back, I'm sure you will be fine.'

As George climbed into the car, he could hear the sound of another vehicle coming towards them.

'Get in!' shouted Leonard. 'I don't like the sound of that engine. It's got too much power in too small a package.'

Leonard was right to be concerned. As the car roared closer, the windows came down and three more of Roman's men popped their heads and arms out. They were waving guns and firing indiscriminately at Leonard's stationary 4x4.

The bullets were coming in thick and fast. One ripped through the metal side panel of the 4x4, then disappeared! The hole seemed to just heal up, just like the car was made of some sort of regenerating rubber. Beth leaned out of the open window.

'Get back in!' shouted George in a panic. 'They will hit you.'

'They need to go back to spirit school – and fast!' yelled Beth. She pointed the palm of her hand at the oncoming car and a bright light like some sort of laser beam shot from it. It engulfed the vehicle, and in an instant all its occupants disappeared.

'Great shot!' shouted Leonard. 'You got them all.'

But the battle had only just begun.

Leonard released the handbrake and pressed his foot down hard on the car's accelerator. With a screech of tyre rubber, the SUV sped off.

They had hardly gone a hundred yards when a very loud evil screech resounded all around their vehicle, engulfing them in the awful sound. As they looked up, the sky seemed to open and wave after wave of blackbird-like creatures flew towards George and his friends. They appeared to have some sort of bow-and-arrow attached to their wings and fiery arrows were flying all over the place. They were hitting the back of the 4X4, but instead of sticking in or bouncing off, they were being absorbed somehow. It was like the rear of the vehicle was made of jelly and anything hitting it just squished into it and vanished, just like the henchmen's bullets had done.

'Let me help,' urged George. 'Erm, what can I do?'

'Sit tight, Georgie. It's you they're after. Stay down, keep safe.'

George lifted his hand and stared at his palm. Could he do what Beth was doing? He pointed his palm at the floor and pushed it forward an inch, nothing happened. He tried again, this time scrunching up his face muscles, still nothing happened!

'How do you shoot lightening from your hand?' he shouted at Beth.

'George, just keep your head down and please be quiet,' Beth demanded in a firm but polite way.

The wave of birds was growing in numbers and the shrieking was deafening. Leonard was driving as fast as he could and Beth was shooting light beams from the palm of her right hand while holding George's head down with her left.

The sky was now almost black with the swarm of birds swooping down at the car. George didn't know what was more frightening, the sight of so many predators, or the terrible bone-chilling screeching they were making! As soon as Beth had hit one flock with her hand-beams of light, sending them vanishing in a blast of pure light, more flocks appeared.

'There are too many of them,' Beth called to Leonard. 'We need to get out of here fast. Do you know where the nearest portal is?'

'Leave it with me. I was thinking the same thing!' agreed Leonard.

He pulled hard on the steering wheel, as if he were flying a plane. The nose of the 4x4 started to pull up and it rose into the air. Beth kept firing beams of light at the creatures, who instantly disappeared in a ball of dazzling white light, while George watched in awe from under the seat. Then Leonard pulled the steering wheel up, and twisted it to the left at the same time, turning the vehicle around in mid-air and they headed straight for the church building – at great speed!

George didn't want to scream, there was already enough noise coming from the flock of birds, but he couldn't stop himself. A faint wheeze came out of his mouth and then it turned into a high-pitched squeal. The 4x4 was nosediving out of the sky, straight towards the church! George closed his eyes tight, wrapped his arms around his head and waited for the impact.

There was an eerie silence.

The SUV should have slammed into the brick walls of the building, but it hadn't. Slowly, George unwrapped his arms and peered through his fingers.

There was no church, no buildings, no more creatures chasing them, just peace and quiet, except for the roar of the SUV's big engine.

'Where are we? Where did the church go? What has happened... and who were those creatures?' asked George.

Smiling, Beth looked down at him. 'Why can't you just ask one question at a time? Why do you always ask four questions in one?'

George looked round at her still in total disbelief at what had happened.

Leonard turned his head towards George, and with a wink said, 'Don't worry. The building housed a portal. That's how we got there in the first place, I just needed to squeeze us through it. Do you remember I explained how we use portals to travel from world to world, or time to time within a world? Well, we just dived into a portal. I dialled up on the dashboard as to where I wanted to go and *whoosh*, here we are.'

'Here we are *where*?' asked George, staring out of the car window to see if he could see anything that looked familiar.

'We are on earth, but in a slightly different location to Derbyshire, whispered Beth. We don't want to say too much, as the world has ears and prying eyes!'

The SUV pulled over at the side of the road. George didn't recognise the area, but it did remind him of his home a little bit. Lots of green fields with hedges and small roads with no white lines down the middle. He could see what looked like a garden shed at the edge of the adjacent field.

'All out!' announced Leonard. 'I think we need to rest up a bit and rethink our plan.'

George, Beth and Leonard climbed out of the car.

'Follow me,' said Leonard, and the three weary travellers walked quickly towards the shed.

He took what looked like a key out of his pocket and pointed it at the shed. The door opened and the smell of fresh cooking wafted into George's nostrils.

'Where are we?' asked George.

'This is what I like to call home. Welcome to my humble abode.'

The three entered the shed, and to George's surprise

the 'little shed' was enormous inside. Full of trinkets from all around the world, and some from worlds George could not imagine. There were corridors leading off in all directions and rooms all along the corridors. On the table in the middle of the room were three glasses, three plates with napkins, and some cutlery. In the centre of the table, George saw a huge pile of freshly baked cakes and a jug of what looked like lemonade with a pot of hot tea and a jug of milk.

'Shall I be Mother?' said Beth with a motherly smile on her young face.

'Thank you,' replied Leonard. 'I will just wash up a little before I sit down to tea.'

George stood there in complete amazement. A few minutes ago, they had been flying in a car and being shot at by birds with bows and arrows. Now they were standing in a garden shed that was about twelve feet by fifteen feet on the outside, but as big as a hotel on the inside! His brain was trying to compute what had happened and make some sense of it all, until his nostrils filled with the wonderful aroma of hot, freshly baked cakes!

George was fourteen years old. He knew his manners, but was far too hungry and excited to bother washing before he got stuck into the cakes. He made an excited dash towards the table, but the firm arm of Beth reaching across his chest stopped him in his tracks.

'How about you just wash your hands first, young Georgie?'

'All right, all right. Where's the tap?'

Beth showed him to a bathroom and a split second later George ran past her and jumped into a chair at the table. Within less than a minute, he was on his second cake, however the pile didn't appear to get smaller.

By now Leonard and Beth had joined him. Through a mouthful of cake and cream, George said, 'Is it me, or does the pile of cakes keep replenishing itself? I could do with a plate like that at home!'

Leonard smiled. 'Just enjoy the food, and when you've finished, we can get a good night's sleep. We have a busy day ahead of us tomorrow!'

George, Beth and Leonard finished their meal without anyone really talking much. Although a lot had happened, Leonard and Beth appeared to take it all in their stride as if it was all quite normal, but George was so tired he didn't know what to say.

So, with full bellies, Leonard showed Beth and George to their rooms and they all settled down for the night. George's head slowly sank into the deep soft pillow, he shut his eyes and thought about the amazing day he had had.

It felt like he had only just shut his eyes when George felt someone shaking him.

'Come on sleepy-head,' teased Beth. 'Time to get up. We have parents to find, don't we?'

George was up and ready in a flash. A very quick shower, a mug of tea and a couple of rounds of hot buttered toast and marmalade, just like his granny used to make, and he was ready for action.

'I don't know who made this marmalade, but it's almost as good as my gran's, but please don't tell her I said so. Erm, where *are* we going?'

'Can you swim?' enquired Leonard with a smile on his face.

'Yes, but what has that got to do with it?' replied George, wiping marmalade off his chin.

'Roman will want to keep your parents hidden – not just from sight, but he will also need to keep their aura hidden. Deep water is a good barrier to put between us and an aura, so we think there is a good possibility they are somewhere underwater. Lots of water!'

'You mean they are at the bottom of the sea?' said George.

'Could be,' chuckled Leonard. 'Are you ready?'

He picked up a small jacket and checked the pockets. 'I think I have everything,' he said.

George looked at him in surprise. Leonard's jacket was a lightweight Harrington type, nowhere near big enough to carry many items. George was wondering what he meant by 'I have everything I need', when Beth handed him a similar jacket.

George felt in the pockets, but they were empty. He was about to mention it when Beth said, 'Come on, Georgie, it's time we moved. Quickly!'

She pulled on her own jacket, and the three of them walked swiftly out of the shed, taking care to look all around them for signs of Roman or his henchmen.

With no one in sight, they climbed into the SUV and Leonard strapped himself in.

'Belt up!' he said as he pushed a button on the car's control panel.

Immediately, everything went white. George couldn't see a thing out of the windows, just white everywhere. It was like they had disappeared into a snowdrift. Then, the whiteout began to clear and they were hovering above water. All George could see was water – it was just like they were in a small ship.

The sea below was a beautiful blue-green colour and the sky above a bright blue with not a cloud to be seen. George felt happy and serene for the first time in quite a while. He looked out of the window, to see if he could see his parents, or land, or anything.

All of a sudden, the beautiful clear sky disappeared as a huge black cloud unfolded directly overhead. The three friends looked up concerned at the sudden arrival of such a menacing-looking cloud. This was not a natural phenomenon.

They couldn't imagine just how menacing the cloud would become. As they stared up, they could make out the lines and armour of a huge airship. The ship hovered above their car and stopped directly above them. It matched their speed and altitude. Leonard tried to accelerate, but the airship continued to match his speed. Then, with a grinding and whirring, what looked like a grappling hook dropped from the aircraft and crashed onto the roof of the SUV, making a large hole in the vehicle's roof.

Leonard slammed his foot hard on the accelerator again, but the SUV didn't respond. The grappling hook was trying to grab onto the roof of the car, but every time it tried to pull the car up into the airship's cargo hold, its jaws just pulled through the car's body, as if it were made of candyfloss. It reminded George of the 'grab a prize' games at the funfair: no matter how good a grip you get, the prize always falls through the grabbing jaws before you can drop it down the chute. For the first time in his life, George was glad the grabbing jaws couldn't get a firm grip.

'We're stuck,' exclaimed Leonard. 'If I go up, the jaws may grab us, and I can't manoeuvre left, right, back or forward, so we've only one alternative left! Hold on, looks like we're going in!'

Leonard pushed the steering wheel forward and the SUV dropped out of the sky and plummeted towards the water. To George's surprise and horror, the big black airship followed them. With a loud gurgle and a sploosh, the hole in the SUV's roof repaired itself, unfolding and contorting back to its original form, like liquid chocolate pouring into a mould.

The SUV lurched back with the force of entering the water, forcing George and Beth backwards into their seats. With an almighty surge both vehicles were speeding along under the water. It was like being in a road race, but underwater. George felt like he was part of some ultra-realistic computer game, then, as Leonard sharply banked the car to the right, he banged his head on the car window and he knew this was no game. The big black airship started firing at the SUV and this time the bullets were coming in.

'Get down!' shouted Beth, 'I don't know what bullets they're using, but they appear to be piercing our outer shields.'

Leonard put his foot down in an attempt to outrun the airship, but it was equally as fast as the SUV. He tried to outmanoeuvre it, veering left and right with all his might, but again the airship was equal to the challenge.

'That thing is very fast and highly manoeuvrable for such a big vessel,' said Leonard as he twisted and turned the steering wheel, forcing the SUV up, down, left and right. It was like a big fish trying to wriggle free from a fishing line!

The SUV suddenly dropped down a few feet as they felt another bang on the roof. They all looked up to see at least eight huge jaws belonging to enormous crocodile-like creatures gnawing away at the roof.

'We're trapped like sardines in a can – a can that's about to be sliced open.' snapped Leonard.

'The roof won't last long at this rate!' shouted Beth, as she sent a stream of white lightning bolts from her hands and three of the creatures dropped lifeless to the sea bed.

George looked around the vehicle for something he could use to defend himself and his friends. It was obvious the creatures would soon be joining them inside the SUV. He found a large spanner under his seat and grabbed it with both hands. He looked around the back seat, but it was too late. He could feel the hot breath of one of the creatures on the back of his neck.

In fear for his life, George spun round, gripping the spanner with all his might. *Smack!* The creature didn't know what had hit it as it fell silently to the ground, eyes closed and lifeless.

'Great shot!' shouted Leonard. 'Now do it again. We will make a warrior out of you yet, young George.'

George was gripped by a mixture of fear and excitement as he swung his new weapon above his head, bashing as many of the creatures as he could. If he had stopped to consider where he was and what he was doing, he would surely have been frozen with fright, but that was the point. He was defending himself and his friends, and he was just doing what he had to do.

Beth used the white lightning bolts from her hands to destroy the remaining crocodile-like creatures and Leonard did all he could to keep control of the SUV. With a sickening thwack, the final creature dropped onto the sea bed, when an ear-piercing squeal rocked the car.

'What on earth was that?' cried George as he held his hands over his throbbing ears.

He needn't have asked. The first wave of creatures had been destroyed, but the second batch were already on their way!

About ten creatures that could only be described as a mixture of a monkey, a bird and a gargoyle swooped down onto the SUV and started to rip the vehicle apart with their teeth and claws. They were no more than five feet tall, but had very muscular monkey-like bodies and man-like heads, but with huge jaws and dog-like teeth. On their back, they had heavy wings which they used to propel themselves through air and water.

The first creature entered the car through a hole it had bitten through the roof. George slammed the spanner into the side of its head. There was a loud crack, but all the creature did was get angrier. The blow had virtually no effect on it, apart from making the ear-piercing noise even louder.

Beth fired her lightning bolt and the first creature disappeared, only to be replaced by several more. The second beast grabbed Leonard's arm. It was hard to see if it was trying to stop him driving, or if it just wanted to tear his arm off. It looked like it was going to do both!

Leonard let go of the steering wheel and grabbed the creature's wing with his free hand. As he did so, George hit the wing with his spanner and with a crack it broke off. The creature screamed in pain and evaporated into thin air.

'George!' shouted Leonard. 'Grab their wings, that's their weak spot.'

Beth kept firing her lightning bolts, while Leonard reached into the pocket of his jacket and produced a ten-inch-long hunting knife.

George and Leonard jabbed, punched, stabbed and kicked at the creatures' wings with everything they had. Eventually, after a long fight with all three friends having received several nasty cuts and bites from the creatures, they were all defeated. For a split second there was silence in what was left of the SUV.

The silence was not to last.

A third wave of creatures was leaving the big black aircraft. This time, they were even bigger and deadlier that the first two packs. This wave of attackers looked like six-foot-tall shiny black robots, not living creatures at all.

They came out of the aircraft and formed a column on one of its wings. They had large gun-like weapons in one hand and a huge sword in the other.

This is it, thought George. *Surely we cannot beat these creatures.* He was tired and frightened, but kept a firm grip on his trusty spanner. He was ready to do what he had to do. If he was ever to see his parents again, he needed to keep going, but what use would a spanner be against such armoury?

'Whisper!' shouted Beth. 'I don't know if you are out there, but if you are, we could use your help. Please.'

The creatures started to move off the aircraft's wing, gliding through the water looking like they were almost flying towards the battered SUV. They were in tight formation and obviously intended to strike as a team. It looked like the three friends' time was up.

Then, with a huge *crack!* the sea bed appeared to open up below the SUV, and Leonard, noticing what had happened, pushed the steering wheel forward into a deep dive and guided the car towards the hole beneath them.

The airship pulled up, completed a somersault, then dived back and continued to follow, matching the SUV's speed and depth. Leonard shouted to Beth and George to hold on as he made for the newly opened hole in the sea bed.

The hole was directly beneath the SUV, and the airship was bearing down on them.

'C'mon,' cried Leonard. 'Just a few more feet and

we've made it,' and with a loud *whoosh* the car dived through the hole.

Immediately they were through, the hole started to close, and with what George thought was the loudest bang he had ever heard, the big black airship crashed into the now fully closed hole in the sea bed. Some of the debris had got through the hole and was on fire – strange, thought George, as they were underwater.

Leonard kept swerving the SUV left and right to avoid the flying debris – it would be a pity to have survived the creatures and the ship's guns only to be smashed by some of the dead ship's burning remnants.

Some parts of the robots were floating past the SUV. Thankfully they had all been destroyed when the airship crashed into the seabed.

Thank heaven we never had to take them on, thought George. *I don't think my spanner would have been enough against their guns and swords.*

Leonard steered the battered SUV through the swirling debris until eventually they were in the clear. Beth looked about the ocean to see if she could find the guardian angel that had saved them, so she could thank her.

George let out a big gasp as what he could only describe as a beautiful young girl swam gracefully up to the SUV, smiling and apparently breathing through the water!

Beth smiled at the girl and said 'Whisper, how can we ever thank you?'

'Just catch the person responsible for so many unnecessary deaths. We have had far too many spirits ending their human lives prematurely as the bodies they inhabit are drowned in my lovely home,' replied Whisper. 'That is all I ask.'

With that she smiled, blew the three friends a kiss, and swam away with a grace and beauty George had never witnessed before.

Within a few seconds, she had disappeared out of view back into the ocean depths, ready to be the first spirit to welcome poor souls who had died in the sea. It was her job to guide them up to the classroom after their watery death.

'Who was that girl?' asked George. 'She is beautiful.'

'That is Whisper, princess of all the oceans. She commands all the waters, seas and oceans. I had hoped that all the destruction from the airship had summoned her to prepare for more souls to enter her realm, and that as a kindred spirit she would be able to help us in our quest. Thankfully, she arrived just in time to take us out of the reach of the airship.'

'Yes,' agreed Leonard. 'We owe her our lives, but where are we?'

The three friends looked about them. They were floating, but not in an ocean any more. They were bobbing along on a fast-flowing river heading towards what looked like a sandy beach. Above them, instead of water or clouds, was just rock – they were in some sort of underworld cave.

The temperature had dropped considerably and the sandy beach was coming up fast.

'Can you stop please, Leonard? I think we're going to hit the...'

Thwap! went the SUV as it plunged into the sand. Leonard pulled forward until the SUV was clear of the water and turned off the engine. The three sat there dazed, but glad the battle was over and they were all still alive.

As they looked around them, it was like a scene from

The Land That Time Forgot: earth, but thousands of years earlier. The land was scattered with big rocks, all covered in what looked like moss. The atmosphere was warm but damp, and there was an unpleasant musty smell in the air. The grass between the rocks was tall and thick, and long, thick vines wrapped around huge trees. George sat on one of the rocks and looked at Leonard and Beth.

'Are my parents here?' he enquired.

'Be careful,' whispered Beth. 'We don't know who can hear us. We must stay together until we are sure it's safe.'

She needn't have been concerned, for after the battle with the creatures from the airship no one felt like wandering off alone! Whoever was in control of the ship would almost certainly have radioed back to inform their master where they were. They knew it would only be a matter of time before Roman's next wave of warrior creatures caught up with them.

Beth was fully aware of what was needed to bring some calm back to the trio.

'Can you make a fire?' she asked Leonard.

'I will do my best,' he replied. 'It has been a long time since I was a boy scout, but I'm sure I can manage something.'

Beth opened the boot of the SUV and did her trick with the food. She unfolded a portable table and some chairs and brought out a tray of hot fish, potato, peas, crusty bread and butter, along with a pitcher of lemonade and a pot of hot tea.

'How do you do that?' asked George with a look of bewilderment on his face. 'Where does all the food come from, and how come it's hot?'

'I am a Provider,' explained Beth. 'All you need to

worry about is finishing your plate. Now, wash your hands in the water and get stuck in.'

George didn't need to be told twice. He piled into his food and lemonade and kept eating until he was full. While he had his face buried in the plate, some hot buttered scones and strawberry jam had appeared. Although George was full, he managed to find a little space in his belly for a couple of scones. *You can't beat a warm scone with hot butter and strawberry jam melting and dripping through your fingers*, he thought.

The three friends sat and finished their meal in a much-deserved peace, after which all the plates were cleared up and returned to the vehicle, the fire extinguished, and the site returned to the same condition it was in before they arrived. No one would have ever known they had been there.

Leonard was just clearing up the last few scraps of food from the floor, when they became aware of an eerie presence. It was as if they were being watched.

Leonard started to wander around in a circle, straining his eyes to see if he could spot anyone.

Thwap! An arrow flew into the sand, right at his feet. *Thwap! Thwap!* Two more arrows landed by the SUV.

Before any of them could move, a group of about eight men jumped out in front of them. They were carrying bows and arrows, and were dressed in what looked like leather skirts, and had painted bodies and faces. They resembled the Cherokee Indians George had seen in an old American western. It may have been a bit before his time, but George loved cowboy films, and especially films that featured John Wayne.

The men moved slowly towards the trio.

'Don't move or speak,' said Beth quietly. She had her hands open to show the men she had nothing in them.

'Wait until we know what they want. We don't want to frighten them.'

Frighten THEM! thought George, as he trembled at the thought of what was coming next. All he could think about was what the Indians were supposed to have done to the early American settlers! *Oh, my hair!* He reached up and grabbed a fistful. *Am I going to be scalped?*

The leader of the group pointed in the direction of the few scraps of food left in a tin on the ground.

'Are you hungry?' asked Beth. 'I would be happy to give you some food.'

They grabbed at the food in the back of the vehicle, but it was obvious they were interested in something more.

They pointed at the floor once again.

'I don't think it is us they're after,' said George, but before he could say another word, the Indians had surrounded them. They pulled their hands behind their backs and tied all three of them up with thin leather binding.

In fear for their lives, Leonard, Beth and George decided not to struggle. It was as if they were telepathic, as no one spoke. They just went along with what the natives wanted, waiting for the right moment.

The three friends were marched off into the forest. Three of the men walked in front and three at the back, while the other two scouted ahead.

'Do you think they are working for Roman?' whispered Leonard.

'I think we will soon find out,' replied Beth.

George, on the other hand, was remembering the cowboy film he had watched back in his bedroom. He was remembering what the Indians had done with the cowboys they had captured. How they had tied one down in the sand and let the sun do its work on him, then put the others in a big cooking pot and threatened to eat them.

Being shot by a gargoyle or a robot was starting to feel like a preferred option when faced with being slowly burnt to death by the sun or cooked and eaten by natives. *How can Beth and Leonard get us out of this?* he mused.

George was letting his mind wander to see if he could remember what happened in the cowboy film, when something struck him. Why is it Leonard and Beth's job to get them out of their predicament? Why shouldn't he play his part? *After all, I'm not a kid anymore.*

Then an idea came to him, but he needed to get to talk with the leader of the Indians to see if he was right.

'Who is your leader?' he shouted at the Indian in front of him.

There was no reply.

'Who is your leader?' He demanded again.

'I don't think they speak English. You're wasting your time, Georgie.'

But George wasn't going to give up. He waited until they arrived at the Indians' camp to make his move.

It took them about ten minutes to get there. George was expecting to find it full of the triangular teepees that he remembered from the old American John Wayne films, but to his surprise they were living in wooden huts on stilts. *Why on stilts?* he thought. Did they have torrential rain that would wash away any building that was built on the ground, or were they just afraid of ants?

He remembered when he and his friend Charlie had been allowed to camp out in the garden last summer, and while they were both asleep in their tents, they were almost eaten alive by a swarm of ants that had crawled into their sleeping bags. He thought at the time that the ants would be his worst nightmare – that was, until he had met the creatures sent by Roman. Now he knew what real fear was.

As the trio were being prepared to meet the leader of the Indians, they heard a squeal and a rumble from just outside the camp. In a flash, all the Indians started screaming and jumping up onto their stilted homes, leaving George, Leonard and Beth tied together in the middle of the camp.

'What's happening?' George and Beth said together.

'I'm not sure,' stressed Leonard, 'but I don't like the sound of it.'

Then an animal that looked like a wild boar with two horns, one coming out of the top of its head and the other from the end of its nose started running towards them. It was making a dreadful noise and bearing down on them at great speed.

'Quick!' George squealed. 'I have a penknife in my back pocket. Can one of you reach in and get it so we can cut the bindings? Quickly, the animal is almost here.'

Leonard tried to reach into George's pocket, but he was too far away. They were tied with their backs together, so neither Beth nor Leonard could see what they were doing.

'It's too late!' shouted Beth. 'He's almost upon us.'

They all gritted their teeth and waited for the boar to slam into them. With the speed it was travelling and the size of the two horns on its head, it was almost certain to kill whoever it hit first.

Whoosh! A well-aimed arrow flew into the neck of the boar. It slowed it down a bit, but the boar was too heavy and strong to go down with just one arrow.

Whoosh! Whoosh! Whoosh! More arrows slammed into

the side of the animal. It was slowing down, but still had enough power to hurt or even kill the trio. Then *Smack!* A long spear caught it in the middle of its back, and with a hideous squeal, down it fell. The trio were saved – for now.

Slowly, the Indians came down from their wooden homes and peered at the boar. They poked at it and rolled it over to ensure it was dead before pulling their arrows out and wiping them, ready for the next time. A couple of the natives pulled the friends over to the side of the camp and indicated to them to sit down and stay there. The other members of the tribe were lifting the boar onto a table ready to be prepared for their evening meal.

The Indian women made quick work of the carcass and in no time the entire tribe were enjoying their first fresh meat for quite some time. But that was the problem – they were eating it raw! *Don't they know it would be tastier cooked and safer from germs?* thought George.

Then the obvious struck him: there was no campfire. Surely a camp like this would have a fire to keep warm, ward off wild animals and to cook their food, but there was no fire and as far as George could see there was no sign of there ever having been a fire.

Okay, they may be frightened that the smoke from a fire could indicate to enemies where they were, or it could burn down their wooden homes, but a properly guarded fire would have far more benefits than dangers, especially at night when the temperature fell.

I bet that was what the lead Indian was pointing to back on the sand, thought George. They had been watching the camp fire and couldn't understand how it had been made and where it had gone. George wriggled about until Beth could get a hand into his back pocket and pull out his old penknife.

'Cut me loose,' he said. 'I have an idea.'

Beth was not sure what he was up to, but decided as she and Leonard had no alternative plan, they may as well go along with George's idea, whatever it was. What was the worst that could happen?

Soon George was free.

'Beth, Leonard, do you have a cigarette lighter?' he asked.

'I have one in my jacket pocket that I used to start our fire,' said Leonard. 'Why?'

'That's a magic jacket you've got there,' quipped George. 'What else have you got in the pocket? Never mind, give it to me quick.'

He put his hand in Leonard's pocket and removed the lighter.

George stepped forward indicating to all the Indians that he was free from his bonds. They all stood up immediately and some drew their bows.

'Wait!' he shouted, and flicked the top of the lighter. Instantly, a small flame appeared.

The native Indians gasped and the bows were lowered. George beckoned to the Indian he thought was the leader.

'Do you want it?' he said. Then he put the lighter down on the ground and walked backwards towards his friends.

'Leonard, please tell me you have a box of these in that magic jacket of yours,' asked George.

While he had been showing the lighter to the tribe, Leonard and Beth had managed to cut themselves loose with George's penknife.

The lead Indian was playing with the lighter and

making cackling noises. Fire was the next step in evolution for them, and being able to make fire was like giving water to a man dying of thirst. The chief knew it would mean warmth and safety for his people.

It was obvious to the tribe from George's actions that the trio were friendly and happy to share their fire with them. The chief therefore decided not to harm them and beckoned for them to come forward and share in their meal.

Beth moved first and showed one of the women how to cook the meat. Having taught the tribe how to cook food for the first time was another triumph for the trio, now all they had to do was to show their new friends how to make fire from rubbing two pieces of wood together as the cigarette lighter would not last long before it ran out of fuel.

It took about an hour for George to show the native Indians how to make fire. Some got it quite quickly, but some were struggling. It caused great laughter amongst the men of the tribe when some of the women could light a fire while some of the big strong men could not. It was hard work, but well worth the effort, and now the tribe were armed with their new skill they were happy to give some supplies of fruit and leather pouches of water before waving the friends on their way.

'Where did you learn to make fire like that?' asked Leonard.

'Boy Scouts don't just help old ladies across the road and take stones out of horses' hooves, you know,' replied George, with a grin.

'Well, we are both glad you turned up for that lesson Georgie. You saved our lives today, and there's no doubt about it.'

Waving goodbye to their new-found friends, George,

Leonard and Beth were soon on their way back to the SUV. It looked totally wrecked and beyond repair after the attack of the creatures from the airship.

'Do we have to walk all the way from here?' asked George. 'I don't think that vehicle will be going anywhere soon.'

'Don't worry about the car,' said Leonard. 'I can fix it.'

Beth opened the boot and brought out a pot of hot tea and a plate of sandwiches. She motioned to George to sit down.

Before Beth and George had finished their second cup, Leonard was calling them back to the car.

'Wow,' exclaimed George, 'how on earth did you do that?'

The SUV was gleaming and looked as if it had just come out of a car showroom.

'I don't believe it. What did you use for tools? Where did you get the spare parts?'

'God moves in mysterious ways his wonders to perform,' replied Leonard. 'Now get in, we still have a long way to go.'

CHAPTER 7

The Three Go to Jail

With a clunk of the door, Leonard was soon back at the wheel and speeding along the sandy road.

'Can we slow down a bit, please?' asked Beth. 'I think you're going to pop my false teeth out if you bounce me about much more.'

'False teeth!' exclaimed George. 'But you're too young to have false teeth.'

The car tyres screeched, and with a loud crunch Leonard drove into a huge sand pile.

'Ouch, my head!' screamed George, as all three were thrown up against the car's roof.

'SLOW DOWN!' shouted Beth again.

'Where are we headed anyway?' asked George. 'Do you have any idea where they are keeping Mum and Dad? Are they nearby? If not, why are you throwing us about? My stomach is in my mouth.'

'Their aura is slightly stronger now,' said Beth. 'I think we are going in the right direction – however, a little more smoothly would be appreciated, please Leonard.'

Leonard continued driving, taking his foot off the gas, but just a little!

After about an hour, the trio found themselves rapidly running out of road. The sandy path they had been following had almost disappeared and they were on nothing more than a dirt track.

'It's a good job this is a 4x4,' said George. 'We couldn't drive through the sand in a two-wheeled vehicle. I remember Dad trying to get through the snow a few winters ago – he had to rely on the local farmer to pull him out with his tractor.'

'You needn't worry about snow,' replied Leonard. 'This car can go anywhere. It has all the traction and power of a...'

CRACK!!!

The car ground to an abrupt halt.

'You spoke too soon,' said Beth. 'What's happened?'

'I don't know,' pondered Leonard. 'Nothing should be wrong. I don't understand it.'

They got out of the car and walked around it to see what had caused it to stop. There was no damage to the car, and they hadn't hit anything! The 4x4 had just stopped for no explicable reason right in front of a huge oak tree. Leonard was just about to open the bonnet to see if the car had engine trouble when they heard the sound of thundering hooves in the distance. It was a noise like nothing they had heard before, and it was getting louder!

The ground started to vibrate as the powerful thundering noise came closer, louder, until the horses were almost upon them.

'Run!' shouted Beth, grabbing George by the arm, but it was too late. In a cloud of dust, the horses dug their hooves into the ground and slid to a halt.

George had his hands over his eyes to protect himself from the dust, he slowly opened his fingers and squinted out. The horses had stopped and the three of them were completely surrounded.

George, Beth and Leonard formed a small circle, putting their shoulders together so they could all see what was happening before them. There were about ten very large black horses with what looked like medieval knights sitting in the saddles. The horses stood at least ten feet tall and their breath was like fire and foul smelling.

The knights were dressed all in black with full armour. The helmets had small slits to allow them to see. Otherwise, the helmets completely covered their faces. Each knight carried a large shield over one arm – black, with a blood-red X from corner to corner. They had several weapons attached to their clothes and some fixed to the horses. A large sword in its scabbard rested against each horse's neck, allowing quick access for the rider. A dagger and a mace were fixed to the knights' waists, and a small lance was visibly strapped to the horses' bodies. A labrys or double-edged axe sat atop of each horse's rear quarter, ready to be grabbed at a second's notice.

These were extremely well-armoured knights who not only had the speed of their horses to carry them, but also the benefit of the high ground, as they were looking down from the immense height of their steeds.

One knight had a red flash on his shield and his eyes were slightly different from the others, marking him out as the leader. Where the other knights had just a red slit where their eyes should be, the lead knight had two blood-red piercing eyes with jet-black pupils. As he stared down at the trio, it felt like he could burn you alive with just a stare.

The knight nodded towards Leonard. As George was just a boy of fourteen, and although Beth was older than her appearance would suggest, she was standing there in the form of a young girl, with Leonard donning the appearance of someone in his late twenties. It was therefore assumed the lead knight saw Leonard as the leader of the three friends.

The knight raised his right hand. Slowly, he reached for his sword, and with a rasping of the razor-sharp blade against the scabbard, he removed the huge weapon and raised it above his head.

Leonard, Beth and George froze. Was he about to cut them all down? To end their lives, just like that? Three lives gone, without a word? No one knew where they were, so their bodies would never be found. All three minds were racing with so many thoughts while their hearts were pounding so fast it felt like they were going to explode out of their chests.

The knight lowered his mighty sword, slowly and in complete control. He pulled on his steed's reins, forcing it to turn towards the three. Using his sword, he pointed towards the large oak tree. As he did so, a door became visible in the tree's trunk.

The three friends turned back to look at the knight, and once again he gestured towards the oak tree with the mighty sword.

Fearing for their lives, Leonard, Beth and George turned towards the oak tree, as they did so, the door in the trunk slowly creaked open.

With their hearts still pounding, they walked slowly through the open door. First Leonard, then George, and finally Beth. As soon as her foot had cleared the door, it slammed shut, leaving the knights outside to stand guard. *Only a fool would try to force their way back out there*, thought George!

'I don't think we should go back out that way,' whispered Leonard. 'Let's look for another way out.'

His suggestion received no complaints from George or Beth.

After a few yards, the path started to go down, slowly at first and then quite steeply – so steeply that Beth was sure she was going to slip. She grabbed onto George's hand. He wasn't sure if it was to help her stay upright, to give her some confidence in the dark, or to offer a supporting hand to him. Either way, he clung onto her hand as they continued down the steep slope.

George felt a strange feeling of being safe, even in his current predicament. It was as if he had felt like this before, although he had never held Beth's hand before. It was very dark, and the further they went, the darker it became. It was starting to get cold and they could smell the damp, musty smell of decay. Water was dripping off the ceiling and down the walls. It felt – and smelt – like they were walking into a medieval dungeon.

By now, it was so dark they could hardly see the path in front of them. Leonard was about five yards in front of Beth and George. He was walking slowly, and although the walls were wet and slimy, he kept one hand on the wall just to make sure he knew where he was.

Leonard felt a thin crack in the wall and heard a faint click. Instinctively, Leonard shouted 'DUCK!!!' as loud as he could. All three dropped to the ground.

Swoosh, swoosh, swoosh. A large circular blade had been released from the side wall and was swinging across the pathway.

'Heavens!' yelped Beth. 'How did you see that coming? It would have taken our heads off if you hadn't shouted.'

'I don't know,' replied Leonard with a croak in his voice. 'I felt a crack in the wall, like a split in the rock. Then I heard a click, and it was just instinct. I could sense danger, and I was right. I don't understand how I knew, but I'm certainly not going to complain.'

Beth and George agreed. They were all still alive and that was all that mattered.

Chapter 7 - The Three Go to Jail

'Keep your eyes and ears open,' advised Leonard. 'There may be more little surprises like that in store, and I prefer my head where it is - on my shoulders!'

The path had levelled out now and they could see a small light in the distance.

'Keep your wits about you. There could be more traps like the blade, and next time I may not sense it coming.'

They continued walking at a much slower pace until they arrived in a large room with flaming torches hanging on the walls giving off a strange and eerie light. There were several tunnels going off from this central point. Each tunnel had a wooden door sealing its entrance.

Bang! The three friends all jumped.

'What was that?' exclaimed Beth. She spun around to see that the door guarding the tunnel they had just come out of had slammed shut

'Oh, brilliant,' trembled George. 'Which way now?'

'We need to stop and think,' said Leonard. 'The black knights are waiting behind us, so we don't want to go back. I'm not sure they will be happy to see us, and I have no urge to face that sword again!'

'Should we put a marker on the door, so we know which way we have come from?' asked George.

'Great idea. Are you sure you haven't done this before, Georgie?'

'I play computer games that are something like this, but I never thought it would happen for real.'

All the doors looked like they would open, but which would take them to safety and what was hiding behind them?

'One potato, two potato, three potato, four - I choose that one,' chirped George.

'I think we need to make the decision a little more scientifically than a playground chant,' scoffed Leonard.

'Okay, you choose then.'

Leonard screwed up his face.

'Erm, all right. I suppose your way is as good as any other. We will go your way, just take it easy. We don't know what lurks behind these doors, and after almost being decapitated, we know they're not messing about. They're playing for real!'

George and Leonard grabbed the handle of the door George had chosen. They pulled with all their might and slowly the big door creaked open. Beth peered through the opening. She could see a bright light at the end of the tunnel, although the tunnel itself was as black and dank as the first one. Beth reached up, took a flaming torch off the wall and shone it down the tunnel. 'Come on, we're in luck, I think this is the way out.'

They walked slowly along the tunnel. As soon as they were out of its reach, the big door slammed shut behind them.

'Aw, man!' exclaimed George. 'Here we go again.'

They inched slowly down the path. The light was getting brighter and they started to feel they were almost in the clear when...

CRASH!!!

Beth screamed, George let out a yelp, and Leonard made a grab for the smooth wet wall as the floor gave way beneath them. All three tried to grab on and hold onto something, but it was hopeless. With squeals of surprise and arms and legs flailing about, the three friends fell through the floor and crashed onto the hard clay surface below.

They all sat motionless for a few seconds, as if waiting for something else to happen. Then Leonard asked, 'Are you all both okay? Anything broken?'

'I think I'm all right,' replied George. 'A bit stiff and my knee is sore, but I'll live. How about you Beth?'

'My backside is a bit bruised and my finger hurts, but I'm okay,' she said. 'How about you, Leonard?'

'I landed on something soft, so I'm all right,' answered Leonard.

'Yes, that soft thing was ME!' groaned George, pushing Leonard off him.

'Where are we?' asked Beth.

'It looks like a prison cell,' replied Leonard.

'Oh no,' George despaired. 'That's all we need. How the heck are we going to find Mum and Dad from a prison? What are we going to do? We could be trapped in here for ever!' He couldn't help tears of disappointment from rolling down his face.

'Hey, don't get so upset, Georgie,' comforted Beth. 'We've been in far worse situations. We just need to calm down, concentrate a bit, and figure out how to get out of here.'

The cell was about twenty feet square with no windows. One wall had a huge barred gate in the middle leading into another pitch-black tunnel. The metal gate had a big padlock that looked old, but still very strong!

Looking up, they could see the ceiling with a big hole in it: that was the way they fell in! The walls were made of a slimy granite-type rock and bricks, and must have been over thirty-five feet high, so there was no possibility of them climbing the sheer walls to escape. The floor was made of big, cold, solid stone slabs.

There were several skeletons lying on the floor in different poses. George had never seen a real skeleton before and felt very uneasy being face to face with not just one, but five. Many of the bricks had been pulled from the walls in previous desperate attempts to break out, but from the signs it didn't look like any former inmate had actually managed to escape.

The friends continued to look around their new cell, pushing and pulling anything they could find that may have been a secret way to open the door, but nothing happened!

'STOP!' exclaimed Beth. 'I can hear something.'

They all stood as still as statues and listened intently. They could hear a faint noise from behind the wall.

'Stand back,' whispered Leonard, as one of the large stones in the wall started to move a little. It slowly grated against the other stones as it slid forward.

Leonard stood to George's right and Beth to his left. They all held hands and stared at the moving stone as it slowly creaked and plopped out into the cell floor with a smack.

Standing motionless, they all gasped as a small man dressed in rags crawled out.

'People!' he cried. 'Where did you come from? Are you real, or more of the jailers come to taunt me?'

The three stared at the old man. Leonard held out his free hand, and just as he was about to speak, the old man blubbered, 'My name is Peter. What month is it? What year? Which way did you come?' He seemed very excited and confused.

'Calm down,' Leonard consoled him. 'It's June 2019. How long have you been in here?'

'Erm...' the old man said as he looked up and squinted. 'About a hundred years I make it, give or take a decade or two!'

'What?!' shouted George. 'We can't stay here that long. How will we find my parents if we are down here for a hundred years?'

'Well, the jail master will come from time to time to bring a bowl of gruel and a jug of water. I have asked many times for mercy, but he just smiles a crooked smile and cackles. He has always insisted there is a way out... IF I can find it, but I think he is just mocking me. As you can see, I have had many roommates over the years.' Peter pointed to the skeletons.

'All have tried to escape, but so far no one has succeeded. We have tried many times, found dozens of secret doors with hundreds of passages leading off from them. Each time I pull a brick out, I look for a door or a lever to open yet another tunnel. Only a month ago, I found a lever that opened this rock you saw me emerge from, but so far it has led me to several dead ends and then in a circle back to here.'

'How have you lived so long while the others have perished?' asked George.

'That is my curse,' said Peter. 'I did some bad things when I was young and this is my penance. They say I must spend eternity trying to escape from this living hell. If I get out, then I can rest in peace. Until then, I must spend eternity trying to escape, to find peace.'

'What on earth did you do to deserve this?' agonised George.

'I cannot say, for fear of upsetting the jail master.'

'What? Do you think he could make it worse for you? How much worse could it get?'

'I see your point, young master, but I'm still not willing to do anything to upset him. Believe me, he CAN make matters worse – much worse!'

The four inmates slumped on the floor to ponder their predicament. After about ten minutes, George jumped up and wandered over to the huge iron gate that sealed their cell. Then he looked back at the old man.

'The jailer told you there is definitely a way out of here. If he is so cruel, how do you know he is telling the truth?' he asked.

'Obviously, I don't, but I do believe the spirit who first put me here and told me I could only find peace by repenting my evil ways. Since then, the jail master is the only being I've been able to speak to from the outside world, apart from the few other prisoners and they were no help to me. So, I must assume the jail master has the blessing of the spirit.'

'What do you mean, the only "being" you've spoken to?' asked George.

'Well, he has been bringing me gruel and water from time to time ever since I got here. I don't need to eat or drink, that is just another of life's pleasures they have taken from me. I have no taste and cannot swallow any food. Still, he sometimes brings a bowl of foul-smelling swill and a mug of dirty water. He has been doing this from the start, and he has not aged either. As humans don't usually live this long, I've assumed he is not human – although it's possible I could have gone completely mad!

'The others, whose remains you see before you, grew old and died. Although I am old, I was old when I arrived. I should have died many years ago. I should be resting in eternal peace. However, this is my torture, to spend eternal life alone in this small hellhole!'

'So, let's think this through,' said George. 'You've tried many ways out, found secret levers that lead to secret tunnels, that have just led you back to this cell. You have moved bricks that have also opened potential escape routes, that again have led to nowhere. Talking to the guards has proved pointless, so you're saying that nothing has worked in a hundred years.'

'That's right, just as I told you, young master.'

'Okay, what would I do if I were stuck in a computer game and found myself in a dungeon or hit another problem I couldn't solve? Firstly, I would ask my friend Charlie if he had solved the problem. Then I would put it on Facebook to see if anyone else had solved it.'

'Well spoken, but how on earth do I speak to a friend when I'm stuck in here? Besides, everyone I once knew will be long dead by now. And what's "Facebook"?' enquired the old man.

'Good point. In a hundred years, you have tried everything, but nothing has worked. Sounds like being back in my world and being left on hold by a computer help desk, then after waiting for what seems like a hundred years, all they tell you to do is switch it off and then on again – like I hadn't done that already!!!' exclaimed George. 'I assume you have tried a three-pin reboot?'

'What on earth does he mean?' exclaimed Peter.

'Search me,' said Beth. 'I think the situation has got the better of him. Either that, or he banged his head when we fell through the floor!'

'No,' replied George. 'When a computer goes down, everyone thinks it is a major problem, but on most occasions it's just a simple software glitch and switching it off for a few seconds and then switching it back on again, or pulling the plug out and putting it back in again, often does the trick. Pulling the plug out is called a "three-pin reboot". I have to do it a lot with some of my older computer games.'

'But the prison doesn't have electricity, so how can you pull the plug out, clever clogs?' mocked Beth.

'I believe it was a metaphor,' explained Leonard. 'I think he means "Have you tried the obvious?"'

Chapter 7 - The Three Go to Jail

Leonard and George looked at each other, got up and walked over to the cell door and gave the huge padlock a twist. It was stiff at first – after all, it had not been opened for a hundred years. Leonard took a firm grip on the top of the padlock and told George to grab onto the bottom. With a grunt and a little sweat they pulled as hard as they could.

Clank! George and Leonard fell back into the room in a heap, George still clinging onto the huge padlock.

'You did it!' shouted an excited Beth. 'It's open!'

'WHAT?!?!' screamed Peter. 'Do you mean to tell me the padlock has been unlocked all these years and all I had to do was just pull to OPEN IT!'

'Looks that way,' admitted George, still rubbing his head. 'Shall we?' He pointed to the passageway leading away from the prison cell.

'Wait,' cautioned Leonard. 'It could be a trick.'

'There's only one way to find out,' George replied, 'unless you want to stay here for a hundred years.'

He moved slowly out of the cell into the dark, damp, smelly corridor. Beth, Leonard and the old man followed him. They were all aware there could be more traps waiting for them in the tunnel ahead.

Peter was finding it hard not to cry. He was finally free but what did his future hold now? He had always thought his life would be over when or if he escaped. Now he was free, and he didn't want to die.

'How did you get put in there in the first place?' asked George.

''Tis a long story, young master,' replied Peter. 'Perhaps 'tis better no one speaks of my wrongdoing for fear I get put back into that prison cell and this time they lock the door for ever.'

Beth looked at Peter with almost a mother's instinct.

'The Creator is a merciful being. I am sure you have completed your sentence and can continue with your mortal life. However, you may be free, but as a mortal you are also able to die, should Death come for you, so be careful how you live your life from now on. All free spirits gain forgiveness if they ask for it.'

Peter smiled. It was as if Beth had removed his guilt and lifted a great weight from his shoulders.

'Thank you, young lady,' replied Peter with a smile – the first in many a year.

'I know I am lucky to get a second chance. I ask for forgiveness and will take care of myself and others from now on. 'Tis my promise.'

As Peter spoke, the tunnel felt warmer. A slight whooshing noise came from above and a spiral of bright white light like many glorious hoops surrounded him. It was as if he had been bathed in pure energy.

'Farewell, my friends,' he said from within his cocoon of light. 'Thank you for rescuing me. I feel safe now.'

And in a blinding white flash, he was gone.

'What...? Where did he go?' said a confused George.

'He has gone to continue the rest of his mortal life, Georgie. Thanks to you freeing him and giving him back his life purpose – his reason for being, for living.'

'My pleasure – I think!' replied George. 'But I just wanted to get out of that cell so I can find my parents.'

'So,' said Leonard. 'Good luck to Peter. Now it's time for us to get on with our quest.'

CHAPTER 8

The Final Tests

They walked slowly along the tunnel, this time watching out for deadly blades swinging down from the ceiling, and also keeping an eye on the ground below. They didn't want to drop into another prison cell!

Leonard led the way again, tapping the floor with his front foot and running his hand along the slimy walls feeling for anything that may be a potential trap for the trio. After about fifteen minutes, they reached the end of the tunnel. Through the dim lighting they could see a metal ladder leading up to what looked like a manhole cover about fifty feet above them.

'Where do you think that leads to?' wondered George aloud.

'Well, it's either go up there and find out, or go back the way we came,' said Leonard, 'and I don't fancy walking all that way back, just to return to that prison cell. Shall I go first?'

Having no argument from George or Beth, Leonard started climbing the ladder.

The ladder's metal rungs were cold and wet to the touch and Leonard had to keep blowing on his hands to keep them warm. It may have only been fifty feet high, but it felt like fifty miles as Leonard inched his way upwards. Eventually, and with freezing-cold hands, he reached the top.

'I've made it!' he shouted down to George and Beth. 'Now let's see where we are.'

Leonard had one foot on the ladder and pushed the

ball of his other foot firmly against the side of the wall to give him as solid a base as he could get. He gingerly raised his arms towards the manhole cover.

'BE CAREFUL!' shouted Beth, giving him quite a shock.

'Okay, okay,' he snapped. 'I was feeling all right until you shouted.'

Leonard decided to tap the manhole with the back of his hand. He knew you should always use the back of your hand when touching things that could be hot or contain a shock. You do this because, if your hand touches something hot or electric, the muscles will contract causing the hand to close around the object. Conversely, if you use the back of your hand, it will close and push your hand away from the object. Leonard didn't want burnt or electrocuted fingers, so he took great care.

The manhole cover appeared to be safe, albeit rather cold. With his right hand on the manhole cover and his left pinned against the wall for balance, he gave it a push, but it was heavy. He braced himself again and gave the cover a mighty shove. It was moving! With one more great heave, he managed to slide the manhole cover to one side and gingerly peered up through the opening.

'What can you see?' shouted Beth. 'Where are we?'

'It's dark, but it is a road – well, a small road. I can't really see from down here.'

Slowly, he poked his head out of the manhole, making sure there were no surprises waiting for him. All appeared safe – for now!

He climbed up through the manhole onto the road above and beckoned for Beth and George to follow. Once above ground, they replaced the manhole cover and started to look around to see where they were.

Walking down the centre of the road, they could see they were in a small street that looked like it was in an old town, something from the 1950s perhaps. The shops were two storeys high with wooden frontages and large windows for the shopkeepers to show off their goods. They could see a barber's shop, a café, a hardware shop and a tailor's shop.

George was looking around for a sweetshop or maybe a McDonalds. Even in the midst of all the excitement he was still thinking about food!

All the buildings were in total darkness. At the end of the street they could see another street crossing. It had faint lighting, like old gas lights. As they slowly walked towards it, the silence was broken by the faint noise of a car's engine way off in the distance.

'Can you hear that?' asked Beth in a low voice. 'I think it's coming this way.'

The noise grew louder as the vehicle approached. At first, it sounded like a big vehicle, but then they could tell there were more than one. The trio froze, waiting for the cars to come around the corner. They thought about hiding, but in an open street where could they go?

With a screech of brakes, four identical cars pulled up in front of them. No one moved a muscle. It was as if they were all glued to the spot. The cars' doors opened and the drivers got out and slowly walked over to the three friends.

They were all dressed as chauffeurs, complete with grey uniform, white shirt, grey tie and a cap. Their eyes were open, but they were cold, dark, blank, like the drivers were all in some sort of trance, almost like zombies!

The four drivers stood in front of the friends. Heads bowed and hands clasped together behind their backs, their eyes were now closed and they looked like tailors' dummies.

George felt his fists clench as he stared at the four men. He looked at Leonard to see his reaction, but Leonard was just staring at them.

George turned to Beth and was about to speak when he heard an eerily familiar sound. In the distance, they could hear the rumble of what sounded like a hundred horses' hooves, and with a loud bang and a flash of lightning, the big black knight and his henchmen appeared in front of them on horseback.

He looked magnificent on his huge steed. Magnificent, but very menacing.

In a deep, growling voice, the knight spoke.

'Well done my little ones. You managed to remove yourself from my dungeon. You are the first to do so. I congratulate you on your work so far.'

'So far?' snarled George, his fists tightening even harder as he spoke. 'What do you mean?'

'That was just the first of your tests. If you complete them all successfully, you will be sent to your parents. If you fail – and you will – then you will remain where you are at that time for ever! Or until I decide to delete your sad little carcases,' he grunted.

'We never signed up to play your silly games!' bellowed George. 'You have no right to keep us like pets. Give me my parents back and let us go – NOW! I refuse to play your game!'

The knight shrugged his huge shoulders. 'That's your choice, little man. You can refuse if you wish. I will move on and you and your friends can stay here in this street for ever. It will be your dungeon. I will explain to your parents that you have decided not to save them, and inform them they can stay where they are for all time. It matters not to me.'

The knight pulled on one side of his steed's reigns to turn it around.

The three friends looked at each other, they didn't like either of their options, but what choice did they have? They could try to fight their way out of the situation, but it would be a hard task to defeat such a big and heavily armed foe, especially when they have no weapons. And even if they did win, without the black knight how would they ever find George's parents?

'All right, what is our challenge, and who are these four men?' pleaded Beth.

The knight turned his horse to face the trio.

'Standing before you are three mortal drivers taken from your world, and one who is not. When you have completed your test, they will be returned and will know nothing of this. That is, IF you get the challenge right! If you fail, at least one of them will die here tonight!'

'What?!' shouted Leonard, raising both of his arms in the air. 'You can't do that, it isn't fair. You can't kill innocent people on a whim.'

'No one said it would be fair,' barked the knight. 'Now, do you wish to continue, or shall I go and leave you all here to die?'

'What—What do you want us to do?' asked Beth.

'As I said, three of these four beings are from your world. One of them isn't human – he works for me. You have five of your earth minutes to tell which is which. They cannot speak. You must use your senses to decide. Your time has started.'

Beth jumped up and made for the men who were now standing slumped against the wall.

'NOT YOU!' demanded the knight. 'The boy has to do it.'

They could sense him smirking behind his metal mask.

'Why? That's—that's, not fair. I know, I know. You never said it would be fair,' she scowled and reluctantly walked back to Leonard and George.

'Now, boy, show me how clever you are,' laughed the knight. 'Let me see if you really are as bright as I'm told... or have you just been lucky so far? If you succeed, I may even let your parents live at the end of your pathetic quest.'

'I hate you!' fumed George. 'I hate you!'

'Good... good...' smirked the knight. 'There is some bad in you after all. That is what I was hoping for. You will make a fine specimen, young George.'

'I am NOT a specimen for you to play with!!!' roared George.

'George,' snapped Beth. 'Remove all bad thoughts from your mind. I know he is pushing you to the limit, but that is his game. He wants to take you into his realm. He wants you to become one of his followers, disciples if you will. You must never let that happen! Clear your mind, think good thoughts. People can hurt your body, but only you have control over your mind and your thoughts. Never let anyone control what you're thinking.'

George gritted his teeth. He now had less than four minutes to save the lives of the three humans kidnapped by the knight and win the chance to see his parents - not to mention what the knight may do to him, Leonard and Beth if he failed.

What would my dad do? he thought.

He needed some nice thoughts, so he let his mind drift to when he was happy with his parents. Happier times, when they were on the beach on holiday, swimming in the sea and the singalong he would have with his mum in the car on the way home. His mum sang songs with him to keep him happy when he was travelling. It helped to pass the time and help George forget that he had a tendency to be a little carsick if he were left to ponder the driving.

Then it hit him. Driving!!!

'Turn the men around!' screamed George. 'Stand them up the other way.'

'What?' said Leonard. 'How on earth will that help?'

'Just do it,' snapped George.

Leonard looked up at the knight, who nodded his agreement for the four men to be turned around. Even though he was wearing a full-face helmet, you could still make out a sense of bewilderment.

George squatted down behind the four men and stared at their shoes. His face beaming, George jumped up and turned to look at his nemesis.

'This is the non-human,' insisted George, pointing to the second man in the line. He felt a huge urge to kick out at the creature, but he knew he had to hide any thoughts or signs of the rage that was welling up inside him.

'Are you sure, Georgie?' muttered Beth. 'Take your time, you still have a few minutes left.'

'NO!' shouted George. 'This is the knight's man. I know it!'

George pushed the man and he fell over. The body made no noise as it hit the ground, then with a flash it disappeared into thin air.

'You did it, George! He has vanished back to the underworld... but how did you know?' asked Leonard.

'I was thinking about my parents, and us driving to the seaside. Dad does a lot of driving. His car is automatic and Mum was always moaning about having to have Dad's shoes resoled because all the driving made the heel on his right foot wear down. But, because he only needed the right foot for driving, his left heel never wore down. So, I just looked at the back of the shoes of the four men. Three of them had worn-down heels on their right foot, but the other man had even wear on both shoes. If they were all chauffeurs, they would have had uneven wear on their right shoe heel.'

'WOW! Well done, Georgie. Once again you have saved the day.' Beth wrapped her arms around his neck and gave him a big hug. Partly because she wanted to, and partly to prevent him lunging at the black knight.

The knight looked down at George. Through the helmet visor you could sense the scowl. Thinking he had given his henchman identical new suits, he hadn't thought about the wear on the shoes. He had been convinced that he would win this challenge. No one had escaped from his jail, and no one had beaten his challenge. He was angry and ready for revenge!

'So,' he snarled with bitterness in his voice, 'you have foiled me once again, boy. I think it's time I put a stop to this once and for all. Prepare yourself for the Ultimate Challenge – and this time you will not be so lucky. This time I will win and your life will be mine, for ever!'

'Bring it on!' glowered George in a defiant voice. 'I will win, I will see my parents, and there is nothing you can do to stop me. Good will always beat evil, you can never win.'

The knight waved his hand and a rope made of fire shot from his palm. He lassoed the three friends and gathered them up. With a flick of his wrist, they had all disappeared.

Dazed, they found themselves travelling through space, bound together by the fiery lasso. It was hot and they could feel the heat from the lasso against their skin, but no damage was being done to their bodies, or their clothes.

They all wanted to cry out, but try as they might, no words would come out. Their heads were spinning and they felt they were going to pass out. The seconds passed so slowly and their throats were swelling up when, with a heavy bump, they landed in a heap on the floor. Once again, they were alone. The knight was nowhere to be seen.

'Are you both okay?' coughed Beth, choking from the heat.

'Where...' – *cough* – 'Where are we now?' croaked Leonard, rubbing his throat.

'Where are my mum and dad?' asked George.

'Can you see them? Can either of you sense their presence? Mum! Dad!' he shouted. 'Are you here? Answer me, please.'

George was spinning around trying to look in every direction at the same time.

'I think we should get a move on before something else happens,' fretted Beth.

'Move on? Move on where?' said George. 'The knight said we would face our Ultimate Challenge, so why waste time? Let's just sit here and wait for him to come to us.'

They all looked at each other, hoping someone would have an idea.

'I think we should at least have a look around,' suggested Leonard. 'Explore a bit. We may need to make a run for it, and it helps if we know our way around.'

'Good thinking, Lenny,' Beth agreed. 'Let's scout around and see what we can find.'

CHAPTER 9

The Ultimate Challenge

The three friends stood up and slowly moved around each other, as if they were doing a dance in slow motion. They started to walk in different directions, which was obviously not what their captor had in mind. They got to about five yards apart when a blood-curdling laugh boomed out. They all felt like a giant invisible hand had scooped them up and, in an instant, they were transported through space and dropped onto a semicircular beach surrounded by a rock wall.

Beth grabbed at George and pulled him towards her. He didn't know if she was scared and wanted him close for her comfort, or if she was trying to protect him.

Leonard had landed on his head. Shaking the sand out of his hair he sat up and gasped. They looked all around them. The sandy beach was about one hundred yards long and semicircular like a big D. The straight edge was bordered by sea and the rear was a huge rock face of granite rock reaching over two hundred feet into the air. Without some advanced climbing equipment, they stood no chance of climbing the rock. Far off in the distance they could see a small island in the middle of the ocean. It quickly became obvious they were stranded with little chance of escape.

Leonard spoke first.

'Okay, sea in front of us and a rock wall behind us. It looks to me like we have three options: try to climb the sheer rock wall, go to the end of the wall and try to swim around the rock to see what lies beyond, or try to swim away to that little island way out there – but how far is it, what horrible creatures lurk in the sea, and could we even swim that far?

'I think the rock face is too steep and too high for all of us to climb, and we have no idea what awaits us in the sea if we try to swim to the island. So, why don't you two sit and rest, and I will walk along the beach to the end of the wall and see if I can swim around in either direction.'

'I agree,' replied Beth, 'and while you're gone, I'll look around for some food and firewood.'

'Hang about', said George. 'Firstly, where are you going to find food on a sandy beach, and what am I supposed to do while you two are doing your thing?'

Leonard smiled at him.

'All right, we could do with finding a way out of this as soon as possible. We're sitting ducks stranded on this beach. George, you walk that way, I'll go this way, when you get to the end of the beach swim out a little to see if you can make out what lies beyond the cliff. We can meet back here in fifteen minutes. By then Beth will have prepared us some food and we can decide which is our best option.'

George felt a little better, and part of the team now he had been given his task to perform. However, he also felt rather scared at the thought of going alone into a sea that could be full of dangerous creatures, all out to get him. Maybe even eat him!

With a mixture of fear and excitement, he ran off to where the beach ended. He took off his shoes, socks and trousers and slipped into the cold water. He swam out for a few minutes until he was round the bend and able to see what lay beyond their semicircular beach.

Nothing!

The sea went on as far as George could see, and it was smashing against a huge, high, hard rock wall all the way, mile after mile. If they were to swim this way, they would surely drown well before they got to the end of the rock wall, or end up smashed against the rocks by the waves!

Climbing back onto the little beach, George looked back and saw Beth standing over a little campfire boiling water for tea and standing next to a small table of sandwiches and rock cakes. The smell of the food made his tummy rumble. He had been so busy, he hadn't realised he was so hungry. With a grin on his face, he jogged back to Beth and the campfire.

'How on earth? Where did you get the table? The chairs? The food?' exclaimed George.

'I told you, I'm a Provider. It's what I do, Georgie.'

George couldn't help smiling.

'You remind me of my grandmother – not by the way you look,' he added quickly, for fear Beth would think he thought she looked like an old lady!

'No, no. I mean you can make a meal out of anything. My gran often made a great meal out of scraps left over from the previous day. She could make a great tasty meal from almost nothing.'

At that moment, Leonard returned from his scouting mission with a perplexed look on his face. His experience was the same as George's: nothing but sea and rock for as far as the eye could see.

'We are obviously not supposed to go around the wall,' affirmed Leonard, 'and we certainly can't climb up it.'

'So it looks like our only option is to swim for that little island then,' agreed Beth. 'Can we all swim that far?'

'I'm game,' answered Leonard.

'Count me in,' said George.

'That's it then,' confirmed Beth. 'Decision made.'

After refuelling on tea, sandwiches and cake, the three decided to take a little rest before setting out on their swim. Firstly, George knew one should never swim on a full stomach, and secondly it felt like a long time since they had all been safe enough to have a peaceful rest. If they couldn't get off the beach, perhaps no one could get to them either. For the first time in ages they all felt a little safe.

Beth threw George a small cushion for his head and told him to bed down on the sand. She would take the first watch. He had no idea where the cushion came from, but had given up trying to work it out. His belly was full, the cushion was soft and he was tired. It was time for sleep. Almost immediately, he fell into a deep sleep and dreamt of his mother, father and happier times.

With a gentle shake of his shoulders and a soft whisper in his ear, George slowly awoke to the sight of Beth standing over him with a hot cup of tea.

'Come on sleepy-head, it's time to get a move-on.'

George came around slowly. It took a few minutes to remember where he was and what was facing him. Then, like a bolt from the blue, it hit him. It was time to swim to the island and find his parents! Surely the black knight would be true to his word and give him his parents back when he and his two friends succeeded in the Ultimate Challenge? But what if they failed, then what? A cold chill ran down his spine.

George was not a defeatist and he remembered a saying his grandmother kept telling him: 'If you believe you can do something, you are almost there. If you believe you can't, you have already lost.' He was not about to lose.

Beth and Leonard grabbed last night's meal table

and flipped it upside down. As they carried it forward, George was sure it elongated to at least double its size. He blinked his eyes in disbelief, but as tables can't expand, and after all the strange goings-on he had witnessed, he decided to ignore it and get on with what he was doing.

With a few cushions on top and empty water containers strapped to the sides of the table, they had turned it into a sort of raft. The legs sticking in the air gave them something to hold onto, and the three battle-weary friends slowly waded out to sea with it.

'Let's rest it on the water to make sure it floats,' suggested Leonard.

Gingerly they released their grip on the table-raft, Leonard placing his arms just underneath to catch it if it did start to sink. But to everyone's amazement, it appeared to float.

The home-made contraption didn't look very safe, and they were all wondering if it was wise to climb aboard. However, at this point, the water was only a few feet deep, so no one was going to drown.

'Success!' beamed Beth.

'Let's face it,' shrugged George, 'we thought we were going to have to swim all the way, so if this thing gets us a short distance, it will be better than nothing.'

Slowly and carefully the three friends climbed aboard their table-raft. They were very keen not to fall in the water – not just because they didn't want to spend the rest of the day soaking wet, but because they were unaware of what may be lurking beneath the waves. They knew that, with all the creatures they had already faced, they couldn't be sure something wasn't swimming about in the water waiting to grab the first one to fall in!

Once aboard, they gently lay down on their bellies

and placed their hands into the water. Leonard on the left side, with his left hand in the water, and George and Beth on the right side, with their right hands in the water.

The table-raft bobbed and floated along with the three using their hands as paddles to keep it moving. Their speed was slow, but progress is progress, regardless of how slow, and it was better to get there slowly than fall overboard and be eaten by some hideous sea creature. And, after all the strange and deadly creatures the knight had already put before them, no one was going to bet against there being more just waiting to attack when the time was right.

They were about halfway across when they felt something brushing up against the table from beneath the sea. All three pulled their hands out of the water as quickly as they could.

'Please let that be a friendly fish,' George whimpered, 'and not one of the knight's sea creatures coming to try to kill us.'

All three friends stared into the sea to try to see if they could see what was bumping their raft.

Beth and George looked at each other and gave a knowing glance. Leonard spun around to see what they were doing and at that point something rose out of the sea and gave the table an almighty bash.

With a scream all three were tossed high into the air and landed in the sea with a huge *spladoosh!*

They splashed and kicked around in the water as they tried to see through the murky depths to see what was attacking them, but the water was too dark and dirty. The sea was full of foam made from the ferocious kicking of legs and punching of arms by Leonard, Beth and George.

Leonard and Beth's heads popped up to the surface

and, upon seeing each other, they stopped splashing and calmed down.

'What was *that?!*' spluttered Leonard. 'Are you two all right?'

'I'm okay,' confirmed Beth. 'Where's George?

'George! George!' she shouted. 'Where are you?'

Then, with an enormous gasp, George rose out of the sea spitting water from his mouth.

'Something dragged me under,' he exclaimed. 'Where did it go?'

'I don't know,' panted Leonard, 'but we had better swim for it before it comes back.'

'No, no. It's okay,' said Beth. 'Look.'

About six dolphins were swimming in a circle around the three friends, making strange but friendly noises. It was as if they were talking to each other, discussing what they were going to do next.

'Grab onto one of their fins,' said Beth through a mouthful of water, 'and they will take us to land.'

'What? How do you know they're friendly?' cried George.

Beth didn't reply, but George could see she had already grabbed one dolphin's fin with her left hand and was making towards another's fin with her right. Once Beth had a firm grip, the two dolphins swam together keeping the same speed and distance apart as she took a ride between their smooth, silky bodies. It was like watching one of the sea-life acts at a theme park thought George, and it looked quite fun.

Leonard and George each grabbed at a dolphin and in a flash, they were also being towed ashore. For once, George felt things were starting to go his way. He couldn't help himself as he let out a victory cry: 'Yahooo!!!'

Within a few minutes they had almost reached the

island. At about twenty yards from land, the dolphins slowed down and the three friends let go of their new-found allies and swam ashore.

Once she was on the beach, Beth looked back and blew the dolphins a long kiss. It was as if the kiss gave the dolphins some form of nourishment, and they all made their now familiar squeaking noise and turned back towards the open sea, the top half of their bodies out of the water with their fins almost waving at Beth, George and Leonard.

'How did you know they were friendly?' asked George.

'I didn't, but dolphins are usually friendly and there are many stories of them helping humans who are in trouble on the high seas, so I thought it was worth a try,' answered Beth. 'The water may have been cold, but their bodies and hearts were warm.'

'I'm glad you were right,' said Leonard. 'They certainly made the journey easier. The distance was a little more than I thought. I'm not sure we would have made it if we'd had to swim all the way.'

'Okay, now we are ashore, what do we do next?' enquired Beth.

'Find my parents, that's what,' said George. 'Bring it on!'

They turned their backs away from the sea and looked at the island before them. The small sandy beach rose up towards a thick mass of trees and shrubs, beyond which was a dense jungle with huge trees rising up high into the air. The canopy was so thick, the sunlight could hardly break through to the forest floor, even though it was a bright sunny day.

'Any ideas?' asked George.

'Well, the knight sets the challenges, so I'm sure he will soon be throwing all he has at us. I suggest we make the most of the peace and quiet while it lasts,' said

Leonard. 'Let's see what awaits us. I doubt it'll be long before he has us dancing to his tune.'

They wandered into the jungle, going slowly but staying completely alert, fully aware they were going to be thrown into the battle of their lives at any point.

'Wait!' shouted George, startling Leonard and Beth. 'Shouldn't we take the opportunity to make ourselves some weapons while we have the time?'

Leonard put his hand into his pocket and pulled out a gadget that looked a bit like a Swiss Army knife, only slightly longer.

'This is all I need, young George.'

With that, he pulled out the knife blade and it slowly grew, inch by inch, until it was a full-sized sword. He pushed it back into the handle and pulled out the saw blade. That too slowly grew into a huge two-foot saw blade.

'This has many blades, all big enough to get me out of most predicaments.'

Beth pointed the palms of her hands at a dead tree. She made one of the white lightning bolts fly from her hands straight at the decaying trunk. In a flash of pure white light, the tree evaporated before their eyes.

'This is all I need,' she said. 'If this can't take care of them, nothing can.'

'Okay, I get it,' agreed George. 'You're all sorted, but what about me?'

'You managed quite well with your spanner before,' said Leonard. 'Would you like me to make you a new one?'

'I was thinking more of a shotgun, a flamethrower or rocket launcher, rather than a spanner.'

'Well, I don't think I can run to that,' laughed Leonard, 'but I'll see what I can whittle from these trees.'

Beth and George sat on a fallen tree and, as usual,

she produced a pot of tea from nowhere while Leonard set about making George a sword from a broken tree branch.

Just my luck, George grumbled under his breath. *Beth has some kind of lightning bolt, Leonard has a multi-sword thingy, and I get a pointy wooden stick.*

CRASH! BANG! All of a sudden, the peace was broken by the sound of trees being uprooted by what sounded like some huge machine.

'Run!' shouted Leonard. 'Whatever that is, it's coming our way – and fast.'

The noise was deafening. Full-size trees were flying through the air, with splinters the size of fence posts going everywhere.

'Watch out!' screamed Beth. 'If some of the debris hits you, it will go straight through you.'

Through the chaos they could see what looked like a massive mechanical spider with huge claws like you would get on a hundred-foot-tall lobster coming towards them, pulling trees out by their roots as if they were dandelions.

Beth and Leonard ran towards George, instinctively thinking he needed protection. They were not wrong. At that moment, a rubber-like arm sprang from the huge machine and grabbed him by the waist. It lifted him high in the air and recoiled back into the machine dropping him into the machine's belly through an open door.

'Heeeeeeellllllp!!!' squealed George, but it was too late. He was already inside the machine.

The huge machine moved on relentlessly, leaving Beth and Leonard stranded in the jungle. They both looked at each other.

'What just happened?' said a bemused Beth. 'Where have they taken George?'

'Why ask me?' shrugged Leonard. 'I know no more than you.'

'I think we should stick together,' she suggested. 'We don't know where they are taking him and we will never catch that machine. It shouldn't be difficult to follow, though, with the size of the path its cutting through the trees.'

'Good idea,' agreed Leonard, but as he spoke the air was broken by a loud screech as two enormous mechanical birds swooped out of the sky and headed straight for him and Beth.

They both tried to run for cover, but it was pointless. The birds were so fast, and could fly with such grace and power, that Beth and Leonard were easily scooped up in their talons. In an instant, the two were being flown off by the birds – but in different directions, and to who knows where?

'Hang on!' shouted Beth, but she never knew if Leonard had heard her, as within seconds she was being carried far away at great speed. Higher and higher they flew. The air was cold and thin, but she could still breathe – just!

Gasping for air and trying to stay conscious, Beth tried to make the bird release her, but it was futile. The mechanical bird's claws were like the arms of an earth-mover – she could never make them release her.

With her mind racing, she tried to gather her thoughts: *Where are we going now? And where are they taking George and Leonard? Be brave. Be brave, my little man. I'm sure we will soon be together again.*

Back inside the huge tree-munching machine, George was sitting in a small metal room, totally dazed and feeling like he had just gone three rounds with Mike Tyson!

What happened? he thought. *Where am I? And where are Beth and Leonard?*

The noise of the huge engine stopped and the tree machine came to an abrupt halt, shaking back and forth as it stopped. George was thrown from side to side in his little metal cell, bashing his head against the walls.

Once the machine had finally come to a standstill, the floor where George was sitting started to whir, and with a creaking it began to open. George backed up as far as he could, but once he had got to the wall behind him, he knew he had to grab onto something or he would be forced to drop out of the bottom of his cell.

He looked around quickly but there was nothing to hold on to.

The floor moved back and back, giving George less and less to stand on with each second. Scraping and rasping against the metal, the floor eventually disappeared into the wall, forcing him to fall out of the machine and down into a chute. It was made of a plastic material, similar to those you'd find at a water park – but unlike a water park, George had no idea where this chute would end up!

Down and down he slid, trying to stop himself by forcing his feet against the walls of the chute, but the sides were slippery and he had nothing to grab on to. Eventually he went around a sharp bend and began to slow down.

Peering through the gloom, he could see a metal buffer wall approaching and he knew he was at the end of his ride. *Thank God the bend slowed me down*, he thought. *But this wall is going to hurt, unless I can slow down some more!*

He pushed both feet and both hands against the wall in an attempt to slow himself down, but just as he was bracing himself for impact with the metal buffer wall, the floor opened up beneath him again and he fell about six feet down into a room that reminded him of a headmaster's office.

With a bump, George landed on a big leather chair – thankfully feet-first, because from that height he could have done himself some damage if he had landed on his head. He fell backwards, and the chair tipped back with the force. Thankfully it was sturdy enough to take his weight and he slid down the backrest until he was sitting upright.

Dazed and bewildered, George looked around him in dazed bewilderment to see where he had landed. Through bleary eyes, he could see someone sitting in a leather chair about ten feet in front of him, staring straight at him. Although he had never seen his face before, he instinctively knew it was the black knight.

George jumped to his feet.

'What do you want with me? Where are my parents, are they here? Show yourself!'

'You have some tasks to complete first, my little man,' leered the knight, who was now wearing a high-collared black robe covering all his body. His face was that of a man in his late fifties, with greying hair at the temples and a long grey beard. He had a ruddy complexion and skin like leather. He was smoking a thick cigar and had a big ruby ring on his wedding ring finger.

'The time for tomfoolery is over, young George,' he mocked. 'It's time for you to face some real opponents now, and without the help of your guardians. I need to see what you are really made of!

'Some of your opponents will be androids, just robotic figments of my imagination conjured up from my mind, and some will be humans I have captured and brought here from your earth. You must decide which is which and kill the ones who are not real, but ignore the ones who are real humans. After all, you don't want to *murder* anyone, do you?'

The knight gave out a blood-curdling laugh through the dense smoke of his cigar.

'Your task, of course, is not just to beat these opponents, but to know the difference between real humans who have been unwittingly taken and are now under my spell, and the foes before you who are part of my deadly robotic army. If you kill a real human, so will your parents die.'

The knight flicked his cigar ash into an ashtray shaped like a human skull, and said, 'Here is a weapon I have devised for you. It is a sword that fires bullets from the hilt. You can use it in either way, as a sword, or as a gun. As you face each battle, it will be your choice.'

George took the weapon in his right hand and felt the sharpness of the blade with his left. Although it was at least two feet long, it was as sharp as his dad's razor!

Happy with the sharpness of his sword, George looked for the gun trigger on the hilt. Staring down the blade as if it were the barrel of a rifle, while fingering for the trigger, George asked, 'And when does my challenge begin?'

'Why, immediately,' smirked the knight.

'Okay, let's get this straight. To win, I must not hurt any real human being, but I must kill anything I believe to be an android, a figment of your warped imagination.'

'Well, yes,' agreed the knight. 'I suppose in simple terms, that is exactly the point of the game.'

An evil grin spread across his face.

'And if I do this, you will give me back my parents and we can all leave unharmed?'

'You have my word, little man – IF you win...'

As he continued to look down the length of his new weapon, George felt for the trigger and slowly brought the blade up until it was aiming straight at the seated knight. He felt his finger tighten around the trigger as he slowly squeezed it. A bolt of red light shot from the end of the hilt straight at the knight's chest.

Whap! There was a bright flash of red light followed by a squealing noise, and the knight slumped in his chair. Smoke filled the room and encircled his body. With a screech that almost burst George's eardrum, the black robe slid to the floor and the knight was gone.

George walked over to the garment and kicked it. It was empty. *Where did the knight go?* George wondered. *Did I kill him?*

He kicked it again, and poked it with his sword, just to make sure nothing or no one was inside. It was definitely empty. Whoever – *what*ever – was in the robe had vanished into thin air.

George stumbled backwards, not sure what he had just done. Where were his parents? How was he going to find them? What had happened to Beth and Leonard? Were they still alive?

As he stood over the empty black robe, he heard a key turning in the lock and a huge oak door behind him creaked open. In walked a tall man, he was about 6 feet 2 inches tall, slim but athletically built, and approximately thirty-five years old, with slight silver streaks in his dark wavy hair.

The tall man clapped his hands in appreciation.

'I must say I'm impressed young George. That was a lot quicker than I expected. What, may I ask, made you think the man was an android and not your jailer? Many people have faced him before you, and to date, no one has worked out that their jailer is not human.'

George stared at the tall man. He was shaking, partly in fear and partly in anger. Should he answer or should he shoot him as well? He decided as he hadn't yet got a plan, he had better play along – for now!

'The man smoked a big cigar, and, from the stains in his grey beard, I assume he had been doing so for many years – or that was what I was supposed to think when I looked at the thing,' revealed George.

'While he was talking, he flicked the cigar ash into the ashtray – a mistake no real cigar-smoker would make. My old grandad smoked cigars, and I remember him sitting with me on the porch telling me stories. After one long story, he dozed off with his cigar in his hand. So I took it from his fingers and, holding it over the ashtray, I flicked the ash off. Then I rested it on the ashtray.

'When Grandad woke up, he thanked me for helping to prevent a fire, but he explained that you should never flick ash off a cigar, as flicking it can damage the body of the cigar, potentially ruining the cigar! Instead, you lay it down in the ashtray, so it can go out safely. Or, if you are awake, you can rest it between your fingers to allow the ash to fall off of its own accord.

That made me think things were not as they seemed. My grandad was never wrong, especially when talking about his cigars.'

'Well, I am impressed, but it matters not! I don't think you will beat the next challenge so easily. Instead of killing androids, I have planned for you a very different task.'

The tall man let out a wail, threw back his head and fired hot flames into the air from his hands. The flames engulfed George, and in a flash, they were both spinning through the air. Then with a thump, George and the thin man were standing at the top of a large stone staircase.

George peered down the dark stairwell, was glad he hadn't been made to walk up all those steps. In front of them was a big wooden door, the sort you would expect to see in a castle or an old church. *Are we in a castle?* George wondered. *Is this where he has been keeping my parents?* He wanted to shout out, but looking at the stern expression of the man standing before him, he thought better of it.

His captor took a large metal key from around his waist and put it in the lock. With a clunk, he turned the key, unlocking the door.

'Make a mental note, young George,' said the tall man. 'This is my key – the only key in existence, and I never let it out of my sight. Come little man, join me.'

He beckoned for George to follow him into the room.

Slowly, George walked inside, his heart pounding and the palms of his hands starting to sweat. The room smelt dank and damp, and he could feel the hairs standing up on the back of his neck. He was frightened, but knew he must go on and try not to show his fear.

As he moved towards the centre of the room, George could make out the shape of a man slumped in a chair, facing away from the door. The man was motionless, as if he were asleep – or dead. There was a large pink stain on his white shirt, but no sign of any weapon. The door was locked and the tall man assured George again that he was the only one with a key. There were no signs of any damage, so it was not a break-in.

Around the room there were thin slots for windows, about six inches across and two feet high, like you would find in a castle for the archers to fire arrows down on would-be attackers. The floor was made of stone, as were all the walls. Apart from the fully clothed man in the chair, the room was empty.

'So, my little detective,' said the thin man. 'We have a body. We have a puzzle for you to solve: was it murder, or suicide? And either way, how was it done? Solve this riddle within an hour and you will have moved to the final point in your challenge. The only clue I will give you is: the door was locked, I have the only key and it has been with me all the time, and when you and I entered the room together, that was the first time I have entered this room for over a month.'

George spun around and faced the tall man. He was angry at being made to play along with yet another challenge with no idea when, or even if, he would ever see his parents again.

'What challenge?' demanded George. 'Why do I have to play these stupid games?'

'BECAUSE.' snapped the tall man. 'Because I want to know for sure that you are the one. The special one. The one I have been looking for. The one I need for my survival,' shouted the man in a very angry and abrupt voice. 'Now do as I say, or you will never see your mother, father or your two pathetic friends again.'

He turned and stomped out of the room, slamming the door shut behind him. George found himself alone to consider his plight.

He sat for a while trying to give the problem his full attention, but all he could think about was his parents and what had happened to Beth and Leonard. Were they safe? Had they been killed? What was he to do? He needed to solve the riddle to avoid his own death and that of his parents, and friends. IF they are still alive.

A loud voice boomed out and echoed around the room.

'You have had fifteen minutes, young George. Are you

ready to give up? Are you ready to see your parents and your friends die?'

George jumped up startled. He had to pull himself together and play along with the game, regardless of how stupid he felt the game was. He needed to play along to free his parents, Beth and Leonard.

What was he to do? He was no police detective, no Poirot or Sherlock Holmes, he was just a kid. How could he solve a murder mystery all by himself? And in forty-five minutes!

George stared at the body. He didn't want to get too close in case he wasn't dead. He poked out a leg and prodded at the man with his pointed foot. The body was cold and stiff, much harder than a living person would be, so George decided to take a closer look.

How was he to work this out? There were no clues, no reason for the person in the chair to have died, no weapon. Could it have been poison? If there was no other person involved, then it would be suicide – case solved. But if it was poison, where was the poison bottle? If he stabbed or shot himself, where was the weapon he used? And where was the suicide note? But if it was murder, where was the murder weapon and how did the murderer get in and out of the locked room? He couldn't have used the door because it was locked. No one could squeeze through the slotted windows – they were far too small. So how was it done? *It has to be suicide*, thought George. *But I must be sure before I give my answer. The lives of my family and friends depend on it.*

He reluctantly decided he needed to have a closer look at the body. He was sure it was just another of the evil spirit's robotic henchmen, so it wasn't a real body – well, at least, thinking that helped George to give it a closer inspection.

He lifted the man's head back and looked at every sign he could see. Then he thought of one of the films he had watched with his granny: Sherlock Holmes, the famous consulting detective of old London and his saying, 'When you have eliminated the impossible, whatever remains, however improbable, must be the truth'. George gave the problem great thought.

Okay, so the answer is here facing me. All I have to do is look at it. Hmm, all I see is a cold body with pink blood stains on his shirt.

Hang on, he debated. *Blood isn't pink, it's red! Unless it's just another trick. Why are the stains pink? Think, George, think!* he murmured to himself. *You have to do this.*

He gently prodded the body again. He was convinced the 'dead man' would suddenly jump up and attack him, like a scene from a horror film!

Feeling he had no other choice, George reluctantly reached out and opened the man's shirt. He could see coagulated blood around a small hole in his chest, directly in front of the heart. *Hmm, was he stabbed?* George wondered. *But with what? Where is the weapon? And why is his blood pink?*

You could almost hear the cogs in his brain whirring around. He tilted the body forward. The small hole in his chest went right through and out of a larger hole in the man's back, therefore some considerable force was needed to do that. Blood had oozed out of the rear wound and soaked into the chair, and the blood at the back was definitely red. He didn't think the man could have delivered such a severe blow to himself, unless he had fallen onto the blade. But, as he was sitting in the chair, he couldn't have fallen onto it... and where is it now? A knife capable of going right through a man doesn't just disappear into thin air.

George walked over to one of the slit window openings in the wall and an icy blast of cold air hit him and sent a cold shiver down his spine.

He put his hand through the small opening and felt the brickwork outside. It was rough where something had damaged it many years ago. He stared at a huge tree opposite the window and wished he was outside. Then he squealed in excitement.

'I have it!' he shouted. 'I have it! I know what happened. Where are you? I have it! I've solved your silly game, ha-ha-ha,' he laughed.

With a loud creak, the door opened and the tall man walked into the room.

'So, what have you, my little man?'

'The man was killed. It was not suicide. Now I've done all you asked, let me see my parents – NOW!' shouted George.

'Whoa, little man, hold on. You seem certain of your decision. And how, pray tell, was this murder supposed to have taken place? How did the murderer enter and escape from such a high room at the top of a high battlement with such small windows and without going in or out of the only door? I want a real answer now, not some childlike magic trick. Remember, the lives of your loved ones depend on your answer, boy!'

'The murderer didn't get out, because he never came in,' beamed George.

'Hmm, explain your reasoning, my little man,' said the tall thin man.

'I looked at the body, and the only wound was a small hole in the man's chest, right in front of the heart and going all the way through and out of the man's back. This therefore had to be the wound that killed him. As the man is sitting in a chair, I don't believe he could have delivered such a severe wound to himself from this position. Furthermore, how would a dead man dispose of the weapon?'

'Obviously,' interjected the thin man. 'He couldn't, of course, so someone else had to have made the killer blow. So then, what did *they* do with the murder weapon? And where did the *they* go?'

'*Simple*,' mimicked George. 'I also found a pink stain on the man's shirt. Blood is red – dark red, not pink. However, if you water it down, it will become pink. I believe the perpetrator was sitting in that large tree outside. He used a bow and arrow and fired the arrow through that slotted window into the man's chest, hitting his heart and so killing him.'

'If that were so, where is the arrow that you say killed our victim?' quizzed the thin man. 'I see no sign of any arrow.'

'The arrow was made of solid ice, and as soon as it penetrated the victim's body to deliver the fatal wound, it became enveloped in the warm blood oozing from the body, and so it immediately started to melt, leaving no trace of any weapon. Because the ice melted into the blood, it watered it down, leaving a pink stain rather than a blood-red stain on the man's shirt. But then, you knew all that because you were the one who fired the arrow, weren't you?'

George felt pleased with his explanation and couldn't stop a slight grin appearing across his face.

The thin man gasped and clasped his hands to his face.

'Well done my little man. Once again, you have come up with the right answer. Perhaps I should have just killed you before I set these challenges and saved myself the embarrassment of allowing you to win. But then I would never have proved to myself what a talent you are, and whether you are capable of being host to the new almighty evil spirit when the master eventually takes over your body. Together as one, you will be able to rule this world and billions of other worlds.'

'*When* the evil spirit takes over my body,' squeaked George, 'but I haven't finished with it yet!'

'That is not your decision to make, my young friend. You have proven your worth, and thus the master has already decided you are to be his next reincarnation.'

'Can I ask one question?' said George.

'What is it?' said the man.

'Have you been honest with me so far?'

'Yes,' the man replied, having thought about it for a second. 'Why do you ask?'

'Well, if you are working for the world's most evil spirit, I can't expect the truth from one such as you, can I? You promised that, to save myself and my parents, I must destroy all fake people and just leave the real humans – is this really the case?'

'I believe it is still the case,' answered the thin man.

At that point, George pointed his sword-gun at the man and pulled the trigger. With the same ear-splitting shriek as the knight's, the man's clothes dropped to the floor and his body disappeared into thin air.

Just as I thought, another android. I have yet to meet the real evil spirit – or have I? he mused.

CHAPTER 10

Someone Has to Die

George looked around the eerie room wondering what was going to happen next. He hadn't long to wait to find out. With a mournful creak, the big door opened and two very large men entered the room. They reminded him of the bouncers he saw on the television protecting gangland bosses.

The men beckoned for George to follow them. As they were so big and he hadn't exactly anywhere else to go, he decided it would be best to follow. He thought about using his new weapon, but didn't think he could get both of them before one could get a shot in at him, so he went along quietly.

One of the men turned around, reached down, and took George's sword-gun weapon. It was as if they knew what he was thinking. *Can they do that?* he wondered. *Can they read my mind?*

He decided to put it to the test. He thought about food, and then he thought about a drink. Both creatures just kept walking. Then he thought about hitting one of the creatures and running away. Again, they both ignored him and just kept walking.

Well, it looks like they are not able to read my mind, thought George. *So where am I going now?*

He tried to concentrate, but he couldn't stop conjuring up all sorts of fantasies, some of which made his skin tingle in fright. With his head in turmoil, he grabbed at his temples as if he had a severe migraine. Instantly, the man at the front said, 'We are taking you to the master.'

Wow, they can read minds, George groaned. *I need to rethink my plans.*

He decided perhaps the best option for now was to just follow and keep quiet while trying to keep his head devoid of any thoughts about escaping, but the more he tried to concentrate on something other than escape, the more thoughts came flooding in. *Aarghhh!* he agonised. *How can I stop thinking before I give myself away?*

Then he had an idea. His mum often sat quietly in her favourite chair 'meditating' – or so she said. George always thought she was just asleep and pretending to meditate, just so she could have five minutes peace and quiet from him asking questions like 'When is teatime?' or 'Have we got any cake left?'

George's mum had tried to teach him how to clear his mind by doing what she called 'box breathing'. It had never worked for him before, but he hadn't quite needed it to work before. Maybe if he tried *really hard*, it could work! Couldn't it?

He tried to remember what his mother had taught him. He closed his eyes and concentrated on allowing his mind to drift back in time to their lounge on a cold winter's evening. He was sitting on the floor looking up at his mother and could hear her words: 'Now, George, close your eyes and take a deep breath in through your nose, taking four seconds to completely breathe in. Now hold the breath for four seconds. Now breathe out slowly through your mouth, taking four seconds to fully breathe out, and then hold it for four seconds. Breathe in for four seconds, hold for four seconds, breathe out for four seconds, hold for four seconds. Repeat, repeat, repeat.'

George's mind was so busy concentrating on his

breath and counting to four that his thoughts just melted away, leaving him to focus on just his breath, the feeling of his chest rising up as he took a long breath in, and the silence as he waited to release it.

Then *bump!* George had almost fallen asleep whilst still marching along with the men and hadn't noticed that they had stopped. With a bump that squashed his nose, he collided with the back of one of the men, who turned around and slowly lowered his shoulders until his huge head was within an inch of George's face.

The guard let out a large growl blowing George's hair back as if he were in a wind tunnel! It wasn't the sound that frightened him, but the awful smell of the guard's foul breath. It was like a sewer and a bowl of rotting fish had been mixed together and forced into George's face.

'Eww! Eww!' spluttered George as he tried to find some fresh air to breathe. 'Eww, your breath is foul! When did you last clean your teeth?'

George looked up at a bewildered guard who obviously had never heard of cleaning teeth. The guard's eyes squinted together as he took a deep breath and filled his lungs with air. Then, he let rip a huge, wet growl forcing even more foul-smelling breath into George's face.

'Watch your manners, little man,' snarled the guard, or I might just forget my orders to bring you to the master – alive!'

George gulped and let out a squeaky little 'Sorry, Sir.'

The guard turned his huge back on George and started walking again.

The three of them continued their walk along the cold, damp corridors of the castle, now with George sandwiched between the two guards. *The walls are made of solid stone and no one is going to get through them*

166

unless they contain one of the secret pathways Leonard had talked about, thought George. *And where are Leonard and Beth? What has become of them?*

George could hear faint squealing and the splashing of tiny feet as if there were hundreds of rats or other creatures scurrying around in the dark damp tunnels.

After about five minutes walking through the castle building, one of the guards suddenly stopped and cocked his ear to one side. George could hear a familiar voice coming from behind a large wall. It was Leonard.

'Leonard, is that you? Is Beth with you?' shouted George.

'George, are you all right?' Leonard replied in a high-pitched croaky voice.

'Beth isn't here. We were taken captive by some large birds. I was brought here, but I don't know where they took Beth. I'm all right, how are you? Have they hurt you? Have you found your parents?'

'I'm all right,' George shouted back, 'but I haven't found my parents yet. The knight said if I beat his challenges, I could see my parents. I have done as he asked, but it looks like he is not going to keep his word. I suppose I should have expected him to tell lies, but what else could I do?'

'Stay strong, George. We will find a way out of this.' Then with Leonard's words still in his ears, George heard a very large smack and a scream from where Leonard's voice was coming from. Then nothing.

'Leonard! Leonard!' screamed George. 'Are you okay? Please talk to me.'

There was no sound.

'Move!' said the man behind George and pushed him hard in the back, propelling him forward.

The three continued for another five minutes until

George could see a large wooden door ahead of him. They were in a stone-walled corridor with no outside lighting, just flames coming from wooden torches hanging from the walls. They gave off an eerie light and cast shadows that may have frightened him at one time. However, after all that he had been through – and his thoughts about what was still to come – the eerie flickering shadows held no fear for George.

The trio approached the large wooden door. The creature in front lifted his huge arm and pushed the door open.

'Enter, boy,' he demanded, and pushed George into the room. The big door closed behind him with a loud thud.

The room was brighter than the corridors, but only just. The walls were also made of stone, but with high ceilings. They must have been forty feet high. There were a couple of windows, but they were right at the top, almost at ceiling height, and had stained glass in them that looked like they hadn't been cleaned for a long time, allowing very little light to shine through.

George blinked as his eyes got used to the light. He started to look around to see if he could find any clue as to where he was. There was a small, low wooden table draped with a cloth and some miniature bottles placed in a rack. It stood in front of an open fire. The fireplace was in the middle of one of the walls. It was about six feet high and ten feet long, and had lots of logs crackling and burning, giving off a strange odour. It was a damp smell. *How can a hot roaring fire smell damp?* he mused.

However, the smell was the least of his worries. He needed to think of a plan, but how could he plan his next move until he knew what he was going to be facing?

Chapter 10 - Someone Has to Die

George stared into the fire for a few minutes to see if he could see anything behind the fire grate. He had often seen secret doors at the back of fireplaces in films – it was where the bad guys disappeared to when the game was up. But sadly, there was no sign of any secret passage behind the fire, and even if there had been, the fire was stoked up so high with burning logs that it would mean certain death for anyone foolish enough to try to get through.

George could see a leather chair at the far end of the room. He was feeling a little tired after his ordeal, so he decided to have a sit-down while he waited for whatever was coming next. He walked slowly towards it, constantly looking all around the room, expecting something to happen at any time. His hands were shaking and he could feel a bead of sweat rolling down his forehead.

I must keep my wits about me, he thought. *I can't let them catch me unguarded. My parents' lives may depend on what happens next!*

As soon as he sat down, he could hear the muffled sounds of people coming towards the room. Jumping up, he ran and hid behind the door. He felt like someone out of a movie: they always wait behind the door to hit the bad guy over the head when he enters the room. *But I haven't got anything to use as a weapon*, he thought.

The door opened slowly with an eerie creaking sound. George could feel his heart thumping as if it were going to jump out of his chest, and his body was shaking with a mixture of fright and anticipation of what was about to come through the door.

He clasped his hands together, ready to thump whoever walked in, but the opening door suddenly gained speed and slammed back against the wall, squashing George between the wall and the door.

SMACK!

George had somehow managed to pull his arms up to his face to stop the door from smashing into it, potentially breaking his nose, however the weight and speed of the door had taken the wind out of him. He slumped onto his knees with a groan.

There was a loud snarl as one of the guards threw what looked like a roll of carpet into the room. *Bang!* It landed on the floor about six feet in front of George and rolled over once.

Squinting and rubbing his eyes George tried to make out what had been thrown in. It was moaning a little, and moving, but not very much. Was it friend or foe? He waited to see if he could work out what it was before getting too close. Then he heard a familiar sound. It was Beth!

Beth was slowly trying to release herself from the carpet. Excitedly, George leaped forward and pulled the carpet off her. Her hands were tied behind her back with rope. She was gagged with a piece of cloth stuffed in her mouth and tied in a knot behind her head. Her feet were bound with a chain that would only allow her to walk in small steps. Apart from her shackles, she appeared to be in good health with no signs of blood, bruises or other injuries.

George was just about to speak when one of the guards who had escorted him into the room grabbed him by the neck and threw him across the floor.

Crump! He hit the chair with a thud, sending it two feet backwards.

Dazed, George stood up and checked his teeth – just to make sure he still had them all! Once on his feet, he turned around to see the guard standing over Beth. Behind him was the second guard, who had a firm hold of Leonard. He was also bound and gagged in the same way as Beth, but he had a bruise on his left cheek as if he had been beaten and his eyes were swollen. The guard followed Leonard into the room, and then came the tall thin man.

'You!' exclaimed George. 'But I thought I'd killed you once already.'

'And so you did, my fine little warrior,' the thin man hissed, 'but as you can see, I live again. What you thought you'd killed was just a hologram projecting my image, so you thought I was actually with you.'

'Where are my parents?!' shrieked George. 'You promised I could see them if I beat your silly challenges. Well, I did as you asked. I won. So where are my parents?'

'Be patient, my boy. You will see them soon. However, when you do, they will not recognise the new you.'

'What do you mean? Of course they will recognise me, I'm their son!'

'You are now, but not for long, young George, for today is the day you become someone else. Today is the day you become immortal. You'll be the king of this, and many other worlds. Today is the day I leave this puny body and become refreshed in your strong young skin, a youthful body that will give me many years of wear and tear before I have to change again!'

'What?!' raged George. 'You can't do that, I won't let you.'

'That is not your choice to make, my little man,' snarled the thin man. 'Your friends are here to witness the death of Stewart Potts, a puny individual who just happened to be close by when I needed to rejuvenate myself. I sent his spirit back to the Creator, but kept his body for myself. His spirit went back in my old body, a trick I invented centuries ago and one I have been using ever since.

'You see, I have found the trick to eternal life – eternal life on MY terms, and not that of some overbearing God! As the body I inhabit dies and my spirit prepares itself to be returned to the classroom of the Creator, I have learned how to make my spirit jump out of the dying body and into a fresh healthy body.

'As only one spirit can inhabit a body at any one time, I have created a way to force out the incumbent spirit and force it into my dying body. Basically, to swap bodies with any human who is close enough to me at the time my current body dies. As the life force leaves my old body, the new spirit within is sucked up into the classroom for "interrogation and reprogramming" into a good spirit and I remain here on earth in the new body. In this way, I can live here on earth for ever, free to cause panic and mayhem whenever and wherever I choose, and no one can stop me.'

He let out a blood-curdling laugh.

'I know there are some special people here on earth. People who can move from place to place, world to world. People who your Creator has put here to do his work. As there are so few of these "special people", it is rare for them to meet, and even more rare for them to marry and have children. You are the son of not just one, but two special people, thus your spirit is far stronger than that of normal human people.

'Today, I break new ground. I intend to take not just your body, but to possess your spirit as well. I have never tried this before because it would require not only a healthy body, but also one with a spirit that is both strong enough to nourish me, but young – and therefore weak enough, for me to control it. I will be stronger than ever and I will never be returned to the spirit world for "educating" into the "good" ways of living. I love being evil, it's SO much fun, and I intend to remain this way for ever, causing chaos all over this and every other world. I will rule the universe and I will do it in YOUR BODY!'

The thin man let out another blood-curdling cry that made everyone in the room freeze in fear.

George shook his head.

'You're mad,' he seethed . 'I'll not allow you to take over my body, or my mind. I will defeat you. I *must* defeat you.'

The thin man laughed again.

'If you think you, a mere boy can defeat me, then it is you that's mad. Come on, my little man. Give me your best shot.'

'All right. There's nothing wrong with your current body. Stewart Potts is healthy. He, or, you, aren't dying, and if you were, how do you intend to dispose of your current body, the body of Stewart Potts? And what will happen when no spirit returns to the Creator? That will ring alarm bells and they will just come and get you.'

'And what will they do?' said the thin man. 'They have already sent their best agents and look at them, bound and gagged on the floor there in front of you. Some protectors they turned out to be.

'No, my little man, there is no escape for you. The plan is already afoot to exchange my body. I took some poison earlier. As the poison starts to destroy this puny body, that is my cue to start working on the exchange. I will join you in your young healthy body and I will totally envelop your mind.

'Your consciousness and spirit will not be strong enough to prevent me from taking over your entire being. At first, your mind and thoughts will be in your body with mine. We will share thoughts, you will experience first-hand what it is like to be a God – an evil, but joyous God. A fun-loving God who enjoys creating whatever destruction and mayhem I wish upon this puny world.

'Because my mind is far superior and stronger than yours, your mind will slowly become enveloped until eventually there is no trace of your former self. At that point, I will have achieved what no being has ever achieved before. Eternal life, to do with as I wish. Ah bliss, victory will be mine!'

The thin man turned his head to one of his guards.

'You, remove his mouth gag.'

He pointed towards Leonard. The guard did as his master commanded.

The thin man looked at Leonard.

'Do you want to see both of your friends die?' he asked.

'Of, of course not,' choked Leonard in a quiet rasping voice, his head bowed, it was as if all the fight had been knocked out of him.

'Good,' smirked the thin man. 'Release his bindings' he ordered the guard. 'I have one last role for you to play, Keeper. You must hold the boy while I start my exchange process. If you release him before I tell you, the guards will kill the girl – in a most luscious and painful way! Then they will kill you and the boy's parents. So, if you want your friends to live, do *exactly* as I tell you.'

'You're chicken,' barked George. 'A coward. That's an old trick, making people do your bidding by threatening their friends or family.'

'I agree,' confirmed the thin man, 'but over the centuries I have used this trick many times, and it never fails because you humans are *so* predictable. Your species may be strong enough, or brave enough, or stupid enough to take punishment yourselves, but you will always give in when a loved one is threatened.'

'You truly are a coward,' fumed George.

One of the guards pushed the tethered Leonard towards George and drew a large blade to cut at Leonard's bonds, to allow him to hold George while the evil spirit made his fatal move. Leonard bowed his head and raised his bound hands to allow the creature to cut through his shackles.

Keeping one eye firmly on Leonard and his guard, George grabbed a large metal candlestick from the table and swung it at Leonard's head with all his might.

Crack! The candlestick made a sickening noise as it smashed into his skull, knocking him to his knees and forcing his guard to fall backwards onto the floor.

'Beth!' shouted George. 'Roll over to the far side of the room as quickly as you can and make sure you stay there. Please tell my parents I love them.'

Then, in a flash George flung himself onto the floor beside the small low table. He grabbed two of the little bottles, one in each hand. He pulled out the cork stoppers of both bottles with his teeth and pushed the open end of the first bottle into the half-conscious and still-tethered Leonard's mouth. Gagging, Leonard swallowed the poison. He was still gasping for breath as a result of the blow to the head, so the contents were swallowed instantly, before he had realised what was going on.

At the same time, George poured the contents of the other bottle into his own mouth. The taste was obviously not good, but he knew he must swallow all of it if his plan was going to work. With a grimace on his face, he flung his arms around Leonard and they both dropped to the floor. By now, the poison was starting to have an effect on both George and Leonard.

'NOOOOOOO!!!' shouted Leonard in a completely different voice. 'What have you done? Now we will both die.'

'That was the idea,' replied George. 'You see, I worked out your plan. You're not as clever as you thought, are you?'

Beth stared at George. She couldn't believe what she had just witnessed.

'George!' she screamed. 'Why did you do that? What are you thinking? You've poisoned yourself and Leonard. Now you will both die, and the evil Roman will live on.'

'It's all right,' croaked George, his voice becoming weak. 'This was the only way we could win. I know the evil spirit has to be very close to the new body when he makes the change. I also know the two guards and the thin man cannot be the evil spirit, as he lives in a human form and they clearly are not human. I had killed the thin man once and we know the evil spirit cannot resurrect the same body once it has lost its life force, it has to move onto another human body.

'Do you remember when we looked into the water from the raft? Do you remember what you saw?'

'Yes, I thought I couldn't see any reflection from Leonard.'

'Neither could I,' said George. 'I thought then that something was wrong. The evil spirit had entered Leonard's body, but not in his usual way at the point of death. If he had killed Leonard and moved into his body at the time of death as he usually does, that would have meant Leonard's spirit returning to the classroom.

'The return of Leonard's spirit to the Creator's classroom would in turn have alerted the teachers and Keepers, and they would have alerted you, thus spoiling his plan. So, he had to make a hologram copy of

176

Leonard, and that copy isn't human, so it doesn't cast a shadow or have a reflection. The real Leonard is locked up somewhere, while the evil spirit is still in Stewart Potts' body, but he has used his trickery to make a hologram so that he looks like Leonard.'

'I have heard of this trick before,' said Beth. 'However, they can only stay inside a body in this manner for a short time, hence the evil spirit needs to capture you and take your body as soon as possible.'

'Yes,' agreed George. 'Having admitted he had taken some poison ready to kill off Stewart Potts and take over my body, I knew if I could pour some more into him, he would not take long to perish and could not put up much of a fight with two bottles of poison working on him.'

George and Beth stared at the thin man and the guards. They had all frozen as soon as the evil spirit in Leonard's form had been hit on the head. He needed to be fully conscious to maintain their holograms.

As George spoke, the evil creature slumped to the floor, writhing in pain and angst, its wretched lifeforce slowly leaving its body. The hologram stopped working and the body returned to its original form: that of poor Stewart Potts.

George looked across at Beth. His head was aching and his heart was pounding as if about to explode. His blood felt like it was boiling inside him. He could feel his life force draining from his body. Although he had only taken one bottle of poison, he knew he hadn't got long to explain before the poison started to work on him.

'When you and Leonard were split up, it was to allow the evil spirit to use the body of Leonard to co-ordinate the final part of his plan without you seeing and to allow him to secretly take the poison. The evil spirit could not have chosen you, because your life force is too strong.

'To move into my body at the time he killed his current body, he would need to be close to me to make the change. He had made the body of poor Stewart Potts resemble Leonard's body, then drank the poison just before entering the room. We were supposed to think he was the thin man, whereas all the time he was inhabiting the lookalike Leonard's body. That's why the thin man told "Leonard" to hold me tight.

'It was at that point I knew Leonard was the evil spirit, and that he was holding me close so he could make the exchange. I was banking on the guards not cutting the evil spirit's bonds too early, thus allowing me to pour the poison into his mouth while he was still tied up. Thankfully my final plan worked.

'I could smell the poison in the bottles close to the fire: cyanide gives off a musty smell like almonds. The evil spirit needed some close by, just in case things went wrong.

'There is only one way we can ever beat the evil spirit, and that is to kill him and at the same time kill all other humans within his grasp, so there is no other body for him to move to. That way, his spirit will have to go back to the Creator's classroom, where he can be helped back onto the path of right and truth.

'He has helped us by making it possible. He brought us into this room where the only humans other than himself were: you and me. It never occurred to him that I, a mere human teenager, was onto his game, so he didn't ensure you were close enough to make the jump into your body, just in case. His total arrogance at not believing he could fail proved to be his final mistake. He gave his current body the poison that is killing it as we speak.'

The evil spirit known as Roman was lying motionless on the floor, dying, due to the two ampules of poison he had consumed. With Beth and George looking on, the body of Stewart Potts gave its final gasp. With a pathetic cough, the evil spirit that had been killing, causing wars, and wreaking havoc throughout the world for centuries, finally died.

George's voice was croaky and weak. He was slowly dying on the floor in front of Beth.

'Now I have taken the poison, I will also die, but that was the only way we could stop him.'

With his explanation over, George slumped to the ground. He knew he hadn't got long and wanted to spend his last few seconds on earth in the arms of Beth, someone who he felt he had known all his life and had always been there for him.

Beth dropped to her knees on the floor in front of George and picked his frail body up in her arms.

'Oh George, you brave little man. You have given your life to save the rest of mankind.'

'Please explain to my parents when you see them. Please tell them I had to do this; it was the only way to stop the evil spirit.'

As he spoke his final words, George's head dropped to his chest.

'I will,' sobbed Beth. 'I will.'

With that, George slumped to the floor. Slowly his eyes closed as his spirit left his body to return to the spirit world.

CHAPTER 11

The Spirit World

George felt as if he was floating. Floating up and away from his earthly body. As he rose higher and higher, he could see the world below him. He could see Beth crying next to his lifeless body. Calmly and peacefully, he continued to float up amongst the clouds. Peering down, he could see the castle far below. The earth looked like it was getting smaller as he rose higher into the air. He had lost the sensation of his body, he wasn't hot or cold, he just... was! A pure spirit.

As he drifted above the clouds, higher and higher, he tried to stop, so he could have one final look at the world below, but he couldn't. He was not in control of what was happening. He was just floating along with no control, but also no fear. He knew he was going to a safe place and he had no concerns for where he was being taken to.

He was now so high, he was unable to make out anything below, so he lifted his head and looked up. He could see a girl who appeared to be gliding slowly and smoothly in his direction.

This has to be an angel, he thought. *Wow, a real angel.* She held out a hand and George gently took hold of it. The angel was beautiful with long, flowing strawberry-blonde hair and a white gown fluttering in the breeze.

They seemed to be speeding up, and in what felt like a second, George and the angel were flying past other spirits who were bunched together in groups, as if having a conversation. Although all the spirits were just white forms, like mist, George was sure he recognised some of them. Some appeared to be waving to him, even though they didn't have arms.

It was all very confusing, but he felt a warm, happy sensation flowing through him – or, at least, what was the new him, without a body. How was this happening?

George's brain was swimming in thoughts. It was all a little too much for him to comprehend. Then, his mind quietened. He knew where he was, he had been there before. He knew he was safe. He was home.

George and his guardian landed gently outside a big grand gate. The angel stayed close to him, something he was glad about. Although he knew he was safe and up with the angels, he still had a little tingle as to what he could expect next. After all, suicide is a sin and sinners don't go to heaven! He had taken his own life because it was the only way to stop the evil spirit. Surely the Creator would see why he had to commit this final sin, and God is all-forgiving, isn't he?

'There is nothing to fear, I will not leave you George,' the angel said. 'My name is Iris and I am here to look after you and be your guide. You may not see me all the time, but I will always be near. Just call my name if you need me. Now, I am sure you have many questions, but first the senior teacher wants a word with you.'

George looked up and saw a kind-looking old man in a sky-blue suit walking towards him.

'Blue?' said George curiously. 'I was expecting you all to be wearing white.'

'The angels wear white, as do the first level of teachers,' replied the man with a smile. 'Then, as you get more experienced, we move through yellow to green, then blue, and eventually to a bright blue when you have reached the final stages of your rise to an enlightened spirit.'

'In that case, you must be quite important,' probed George.

'Oh, I suppose you could say that,' chuckled the old man. 'However, enough discussion about this place and its ways. It is not yet ready for you, nor you for it. The Creator has spoken to me and he has made a decision he has never made before – and believe me there have been many worthy opportunities over the centuries.

'We believe you are aware of the magnitude of your actions and the sacrifice you have made. We believe you made a decision based on pure love for your family and the need for all mankind to be free from this evil spirit.

'Your sacrifice enabled you to accomplish what we have been unable to do for many years: you have made it possible for us to return the evil spirit we know as Roman to our classrooms where he will be unable to wreak any further havoc, allowing our teachers to teach him the true ways. In doing so, you have saved many millions of lives and prevented far more spirits from being turned away from the true light and salvation.

'You have completed a deed of great magnitude and of much importance to the whole of humankind and the spirit world. Over the years, many have tried to accomplish what you have done, but all have failed. Now, we have the evil spirit on his way back to the spirit world where we can contain him long enough to remove all evil from his pneuma and turn him back into the kind spirit he was always meant to be.

'So, young George Thomson. For the first time in history the Creator has given a mortal a second chance at life on earth. He will return you to the earthly world, back to your family where you can live out your human life and use your free will to make the free decisions all humans are able to choose in living your lives. When your time finally comes, you will return here, as do all spirits, and you will be held to account for what you have done so far and what you have left to do.

'On behalf of the Creator of all things, living or otherwise, I thank you, George Thomson, and say: "Go now and enjoy your life. Live it to the fullest, and remember: you get out of life what you put in."

'Real happiness comes from giving, and you were prepared to give your life for the rest of mankind, so now you can go back and return to your mortal life. I am sure you will have many more adventures, and a long and enjoyable life.'

George had many questions, but as soon as the old man had finished speaking, he vanished.

George found himself being whisked up, like he was a puff of smoke being sucked up into a vacuum cleaner. His spirit was falling through space, gently but quickly. Suddenly, he could see clouds, then the sky beneath them, his body below him and Beth sitting as she had been in front of his lifeless form.

Beth was looking down on the body of George. Tears filled her eyes and some were dripping onto his face.

George coughed, spluttered, then opened his eyes and his body sat up in a start. He was back inside his own body. No damage. No bruises. He felt great. Dazed and confused, but it was great to be alive again.

'George!' screamed Beth. 'You... you... you're ALIVE!!! But I watched you die! What happened?'

'I-I-I-I have been to heaven, I think. I was met by an angel called Iris and she took me to see an old man who said I could have my life back for helping mankind. At least, I think that's what happened. Or was I dreaming? It felt real, but then dreams do, don't they?'

Beth grabbed George and gave him a big hug that

seemed to go on forever.

'I think we need to find your parents and the real Leonard, then we need to get out of here. This place gives me the creeps. Do you feel up to it? Are you ready to get out of here? Can you walk?'

'Lead the way,' said George with a smile.

The two of them started wandering through the castle, shouting out for Leonard and George's parents.

'Mum! Dad! Leonard! Can you hear us? Where are you?' yelled George.

They stopped shouting when they heard a muffled sound coming from the other side of a wall.

It was a humming sound with a rhythmic beat.

'I know that sound,' exclaimed George. 'It's a photocopier. Dad has one in his office. I was not allowed in when he or Mum were working, but I used to hear it when I was playing downstairs.'

George looked at Beth with a puzzled expression on his face. *Who on earth is photocopying in a castle? What is going on? Where are we?* he wondered.

George stared at Beth. As he looked at her face, it appeared to change. Her features seemed to morph into an older face, then back again.

'Beth, what's happening? Where are we?'

George felt cold, then hot. His body shook and made his eyes close, just for a second. When he looked around him, he was sitting in his grandmother's kitchen. Leonard and his Granny were standing over him, and his mum and dad were walking through the door. He jumped up and grabbed both his parents. His eyes were crying with pure pleasure and excitement.

For what seemed like an eternity, George and his parents hugged and kissed each other.

'Where have you been? How are you? Why couldn't

you escape? Did Roman hurt you?' he enquired.

'Calm down, George,' beamed his mother. 'We are all safe, thanks to you. There is plenty of time for us to explain what happened to us, and we want to know all about your adventure and how you managed to free us from Roman and his army.'

Then George turned to Leonard.

'How are you Leonard? What did they do to you? And where's Beth?'

'I'm here, Georgie,' said his grandmother.

'What?!' exclaimed George. 'No, I meant Beth, Granny. Young Beth, not you.'

'I am Beth, George – or I was once. I am Elizabeth. I'm your grandmother in this time, but before you were born Leonard and I had many adventures helping the spirits keep the peace.

'When your parents were taken, we knew Roman had his mind set on you and it was only a matter of time before he came for you. When we knew he was close, Leonard was sent to protect you. However, the spirits kept an eye on your progress and when you were both captured, I was sent to help, although I agree you didn't need much protecting.

'You did very well, Georgie. You have had an amazing adventure – the adventure of a lifetime – but I think it is just the start of many. You have proven your worth and I am sure the spirit world will be in need of your talents again.'

George looked at his granny with a beaming smile.

'Do you know what I'm thinking?' he asked her.

'Why of course,' she answered. 'You're thinking "I'm hungry. What can Granny have in her larder?" Look behind you, Georgie.'

George turned around to see the table full of food,

hot chicken and hot pies, roast vegetables, fruits, cheese and breads of all kinds and racks of all sorts of cake. A pot full of tea, chocolate ice cream, lemonade and enough big, comfy seats for everyone.

'I love you, Granny,' said George with a huge smile all across his face.

As he tucked into the fabulous spread for all he was worth, Elizabeth looked out of the window towards the skies. Way up high, far above the clouds, some previously earthbound spirits had left their mortal bodies and were rising high in the sky, returning to the spirit world to be greeted by their own personal teacher who as always would be ready to welcome them back home.

While all the spirits were now in their spirit smoke-like form with no discernable features to the human eye, one stood out from the rest. It was as if this spirit were a little darker than all the others, and it almost had eyes – little red eyes staring through the smokey haze, staring back at the earth below, staring straight at... George.